survival
tips
stories

MIRIAM GERSHOW

PROPELLER BOOKS • PORTLAND, OR

These stories have been previously published in the following publications: "Little Girl" in *The Journal*; "Carker" in *The Georgia Review* and *The Robert Olen Butler Prize Stories*; "All That Apply" in *Pithead Chapel*; "Congratulations, Baby" in *Quarterly West*; "Survival Tips: Toddler Birthday Party" in *Pidgeonholes*; "Big Home" (as "A Step Ahead") in *Black Warrior Review*; "Lines of Communication" in *Variant Lit* and *Already Gone (Alan Squire Books)*; "Don't Leave Me" in *Gulf Coast*; "The Book of Adornments" in *Rejection Letters*.

Cover and interior design by Dan DeWeese

Published by Propeller Books, Portland, Oregon.
ISBN 978-1-955593-08-3

www.propellerbooks.com

In memory of
Irwin Gershow and Cai Emmons
who I hope are trading lessons in kvetching and contentment

contents

little girl

MY BEST FRIEND'S FATHER fell in love with one of his students from the community college. We were sixteen at the time. The girlfriend was twenty-two. Polly called me when she found out. *This is not about how much I love you,* her dad had told her. *These things happen. They're unexpected. We can't plan for everything.* His face, she said, puffed up while he was talking like he had the mumps. His nose turned red and started to run, and his fingers squeezed her knee until it hurt.

"Maybe you'll get to paint your room," I said.

When our friend Kathleen's dad moved out, her mom let her paint her room any color she wanted. Divorce had become fashionable in our neighborhood. It was like a fever, starting quietly enough in one private corner of town, then spreading wildly through the streets. Separations. Court cases. Child support. Alimony. Weekend visitations. Dads living in antiseptic beige apartments in nearby cities.

Polly didn't say anything. I could hear strained breathing in the phone.

"Sorry," I said. "I was just kidding."

"I don't know what to do," she said and then talked for a long time. Her parents had screamed at each other for three hours. Her dad could get fired, she said. Her mom was locked in the bedroom and wouldn't come out. *He's leaving*, Polly kept repeating. I tried to feel bad but I found the whole thing exciting, electric. Fifty-two pick-up; all the cards thrown in the air, flitting down to the ground in a scattered mess.

In my own home, there was a lulling sameness. My father read the *New York Times* or thumbed through his classical music collection, blowing dust off the records as he pulled them from their sleeves. My mother sat working on one of her half-finished needlepoints, resting it on the couch cushions if she went to cook dinner or move the laundry to the dryer, the needle safely hooked through a few holes so it wouldn't accidentally poke someone. They rarely fought. They rarely held hands. I listened at night to their heavy footsteps up the stairs to bed, my mother first, just past dark, then my father an hour or two later.

Dinners were a slow round robin of my father asking my mother about her day, my mother asking him back, both of them then turning to me. When I spoke, I watched their faces and wondered if they were doing the same thing I did in American history class, pressing their fingernails to the insides of their palms so they'd remember to listen. Sometimes, as I brought water glasses from the sink—ice for my father, no ice for my mother and me—I imagined myself as a waitress, these people as my diners. They would be the couple in the corner of the restaurant who I would quickly forget as soon as I turned away. They would sit quietly, unprotesting and hungry, while I waited on noisier families and kissing couples.

"My mother threw a plate at him," Polly said. "And then a coffee mug."

"Where's he now?"

"Left. Probably at his girlfriend's." With the last word, she started crying. I tried to imagine the whole thing, Mrs. Lastrem sprawled across her bedspread, shoulders shaking, red-faced, not even bothering to wipe the snot from her nose. Mr. Lastrem weaving in and out of traffic, his wet armpits leaving dark rings in his button-down, hitting his horn once, then again, trying to push the cars forward in his frenzied rush to his student's house. The shards of china scattered in a messy pile along the linoleum.

Our friend Kathleen had picked hot pink for her room. And she'd painted it herself, streaking the walls unevenly, with thick drops of dried paint everywhere, making the whole thing look speckled. A string of plastic beads hung in her doorway. The walls gave her a headache sometimes, but when she complained, her mom said, "Your bed. You lie in it." Since her dad left, Kathleen's mom wore tight denim dresses or shimmering tank tops and miniskirts. The skin of her arms hung wobbly and loose, and her legs had thick blue veins. But I liked how she piled all her hair on top of her head and held it in place with shiny gold clips and combs. Whenever I went there, the house smelled odd, like something had just been burnt. Both doors were usually open, even if no one was on the first floor, and the wind blew through the entryways, the screen doors rattling against the house. You had to yell "Hello? Hello?" until you found someone. One time, no one was home and the doors were like that. I didn't close them on my way out, just left like I'd never even been there.

I wondered if Polly's house would be like that now, a place where anything could happen.

Her breath steadied in the phone, and she started to say something, but her mother yelled in the background. I couldn't make out the words, but the sound was high-pitched and jagged. "I gotta go," Polly said and rushed off the phone. After I hung up, my cheeks got warm and my chest tightened. I wasn't used to being jealous of Polly.

The next day after school, she made me go with her to the community college, so we could sit in her car and point to girls walking along the grass, trying to guess which one it was. Polly kept picking the most beautiful, tall, longhaired blondes with halter-tops and skintight jeans, chunky-heeled shoes. I thought it was probably a more bookish girl, one who held her bag across her chest, wore glasses and tied her hair in a bun. Mr. Lastrem was not a good-looking man. He had a plump, pale face with dark half-moon bags under his eyes. Polly had his face. In elementary school, some of the boys had called her Pillsbury. Even in high school, no one had kissed her yet. Three boys had already been down my pants by the middle of our sophomore year.

"That one," she said, picking a beautiful amber-haired girl in a sleeveless red dress. The material was gauzy and flowing, ending just above her knees. She had huge boobs. It was too cold for the dress, barely any leaves on the trees yet, and the girl's nipples poked through the fabric like two fingers leading the way.

"Oh right," I said and laughed.

Polly looked at me like I'd slapped her, eyebrows bunched together, her mouth in a small *o*. I had to be careful with Polly. There was something about her flat smile, the way she licked her lips until they chapped, how she wheezed softly while she ate, that made me want to be mean to her. And she would let me. I knew that; the knowledge only made me meaner. One time I had stopped speaking to her for a week, because I liked the messy, urgent notes she sent begging for my forgiveness for whatever she'd done wrong. I would watch her watching me in the cafeteria, sitting by herself while I sat at a table full of other girls. I'd laugh extra hard, throw my head back and make a loud noise, flipping my hair in a way that made it bounce against my shoulders. I felt vaguely guilty, but more than that, I wanted her to keep staring at me from across the room. I didn't know what to call it at the time, but in her panic and her need, Polly looked at me like someone in love.

The red dress girl was almost out of sight, moving quickly behind one of the long concrete buildings. I petted Polly's leg. "Yeah, maybe that's her," I said. "She's pretty."

Polly's eyes pooled with water. She'd started wearing make-up recently and the mascara clumped her eyelashes together. The blue eye shadow was a few shades too light. When the tears fell, they streaked her skin with a messy brown.

"It'll be okay," I said. It was hard for me to picture Mr. Lastrem, who taught calculus and came home with chalk in his hair, who wore faded suit jackets with suede elbow patches, who got spaghetti sauce caught in his mustache, as the cause of all of this. It titillated me, the idea of unknown passions and hidden drama, of Mr. Lastrem's pudgy face buried in the breasts of a tiny girl as she called out his name.

Polly's crying caught in her throat, and she made a gasping noise. She brought her hand to her mouth, as if the sound had surprised her.

"It'll be okay," I said again, but Polly didn't answer. She started the car and drove us back through the neighborhood. I knew I should have touched her, maybe stroked her hair or squeezed her shoulder, said something nice. But I couldn't. It was like he was there between us, Mr. Lastrem, me looking at him from one side and Polly from the other, each of us seeing something completely different, neither knowing how to reach around.

At dinner, I said to my parents, "Polly's dad is having an affair."

We were eating teriyaki chicken. My father had bought my mother an international cookbook for her last birthday, *Recipes From Around the Globe*, and teriyaki was one of her favorites. We had all been quiet for a while before I said, *Polly's dad is having an affair*. I had repeated the sentence over and over in my head before I spoke. Practicing, because sometimes breaking through their quiet was like punching through a wall; it needed momentum. It was not an angry or sullen silence at our table. My mother often sat dabbing her lips with her napkin, my father cutting his food into small pieces. There was no tension. Quiet was how they liked it.

"Polly's dad is having an affair," I said.

My mother looked at me. "Okay," she said.

"Okay?" It seemed like an absurd thing for her to say.

"How do you know?" she said.

"Polly told me."

"Well, you can't believe every rumor you hear."

"It's not a rumor. Polly told me herself. Her dad told her. Her mom threw stuff at him." My voice was rising. "It's one of his students. He's sleeping with some twenty-two-year-old from his math class."

My mother stared at me. My father was still eating his chicken. I waited for either of them to speak.

Sometimes I spilled things on purpose, knocking over the gravy boat or a glass of orange soda. I liked how everyone jumped, all of us moving at once, hands and arms and voices jumbled together for a second, color spreading across the checked tablecloth. In that moment, everyone was as noisy and restless as me.

"Well, that's too bad," my mother said. I waited for more—even though I knew none would come—until we were all quiet again.

I brought Kathleen the next time we went to the community college.

"Why?" Polly had whispered when she saw Kathleen walking down the hall toward our lockers. Polly didn't like Kathleen.

"It'll be fun," I said. I smiled big and shoved her shoulder. "Come on."

Kathleen sat in the backseat, holding her cigarette out the window. "You can't do that in here," Polly had said when Kathleen lit the first one. Kathleen took a long drag before rolling down the window. Her hand rested just outside the glass, and most of the smoke blew back into the car. Polly didn't say anything else about it.

"There," Polly said and pointed. It was her typical choice. Thick blonde hair held back in two barrettes, light eyes, perfect posture, a pointy little nose. She wore a cropped cardigan over a tube dress. The girl swayed her hips when she walked, in a way that made it look like she knew something about the world.

"How 'bout her?" Kathleen said, pointing to a middle-aged Black lady with a tall afro. She laughed, and I did too.

"Not funny," Polly said.

Kathleen leaned her head into the front seat, her mouth smelling of smoke when she talked. "Why do you think he started banging her?"

Polly looked at me. She never knew how to talk to Kathleen. The only way to shut Kathleen up was by getting right back in her face. But Polly didn't know how to, or wasn't capable, or both.

"I have no idea," Polly said, looking at her hands.

"Do your mom and dad still have sex? I mean, did they before all this shit started?"

Polly cleared her throat. For a moment, I thought she was going to say something, grew certain of it, but nothing came. I wanted to shake the words out of her; it was deadening, watching her do nothing. She put her hands on the steering wheel, at ten o'clock and two o'clock, gripping so hard her knuckles turned white.

"Sit back," I said to Kathleen. "Your breath stinks."

"Fuck off," Kathleen said as she moved.

I smiled at Polly, but she was squinting out the window. I patted the hand at two o'clock, brushing my fingers over her knuckles. She kept staring. No one was walking by, but even so, she acted like there was something fascinating going on.

"There's your boyfriend, Sara," Kathleen said, pointing out the back window to a boy in the parking lot. He was tall and red-faced with a silvery mouth full of braces. Strands of stringy hair reached halfway down his back. He walked with his shoulders hunched forward.

"I stole him away from you," I said.

"I could rock his fucking world," she said. "I bet he's got a pencil dick though. There's nothing worse than a pencil dick." Kathleen had slept with a bunch of guys. She liked to talk about penises. She had a million names—cock dick prick rod stick shaft pole. For a while she called them cocker spaniels. *I rode his spaniel for so long*, she'd say, *my legs started to cramp*. She showed me hickeys, running her fingers around and around the speckled bruises.

When the first guy, Seth Landry, went down my pants, I called Kathleen afterwards. "How many fingers did he use?" she asked.

"I don't know."

"How can you not know? Was it just his pinkie or a whole fistful?"

"Closer to a fistful," I said.

"Did it hurt or feel good?"

"Good," I lied. I didn't want her to think I was a prude.

"Did he touch your tits?"

"Yeah."

"How? Did he rub them or suck them or what?"

Her questions came rapid-fire. I liked answering, even though it felt stupid at first. Saying the words prolonged the whole thing, made it seem sophisticated and dirty and mine. Kathleen made approving noises when I told her details, like how he'd held his fingers under my nose when he finished, asking if I liked the smell. "Did you?" Kathleen said. She seemed hungry and unafraid to show it. I told her his prick was stiff in his pants and he kept rubbing it against me. "His battering ram," she called it and laughed.

Kathleen and I talked about it for days, different versions, different moments, until the story felt softened and worn, like a piece of paper kept in a pocket too long. There were some things I didn't tell her. Before Seth started using his fingers, when he was still just kissing me and running his hands over the outside of my clothes, I had felt a fevered rush. All of my senses were alert but disoriented from his hot breath on my face and the taste of him in my mouth. I felt like crying, not sure if I was really happy or really sad. He kept whispering in my ear, *you're so pretty* and I liked how the *puh* sound popped in the air. When it began to hurt, I didn't stop him because I didn't want him to go away.

Kathleen lit another cigarette from the backseat, and Polly shook her head.

"Let's find Polly's boyfriend now," Kathleen said, blowing smoke into the front seat. Polly bit the inside of her cheek. She always did that when she was nervous, ate the inside of her mouth until it was bloodied and raw.

"Poll–" I said.

She was shaking her head, barely at all, only the tiniest of motions, but I could see. She started the car quickly, and when she backed out of the parking space, the tires made a sharp squealing noise.

"Whoa!" Kathleen yelled.

A girl on the sidewalk watched us, one hand to her throat, looking startled by the noise. She was short and slightly overweight and held a long corduroy jacket closed over her shirt. She'd combed out her curly hair and it hung in frizzy chunks on both sides. In a crowd, my eyes would have passed right over her. I wondered what would happen if this turned out to be Mr. Lastrem's girlfriend, if this was the type of girl he'd leave Polly for.

There were short black tire marks on the cement, angry streaks left in our parking space.

"I'm sorry," I could have said to Polly. Neither of us spoke, and when Kathleen started her monologue about how many traffic accidents are caused by reckless driving, no one told her to quiet down.

Mr. Lastrem moved out. He backed a U-Haul into the driveway, Polly said, and shoveled his stuff into the back of the truck. Nothing was packed; he threw his clothes into garbage bags and carried books by the armful. His new apartment was in Leland Heights, three miles away, with a big brown

couch that smelled of mildew and a television that sat on
the floor and only got a couple of channels, even with the
antennae. When Polly visited, they watched fuzzy PBS while
Mr. Lastrem drank martinis, and she drank seltzer since he
hadn't remembered to buy juice or pop or milk.

In the beginning, her house didn't seem different. The first
time I went over, there was still the L-shaped couch in the
living room, the fake wood entertainment center with the
TV and stereo, the old kitchen table nicked around the edges
and the goldfish-patterned shower curtain. In the hallway,
though, there were blank spots where pictures used to hang,
rectangles of clean white paint standing against the dingier
gray of the rest of the wall.

"She took down all his pictures," Polly said.

I had never realized how dirty the wall was before. The
contrast was dramatic, and there was something satisfying
about the sight. It seemed to me exactly how a wall should
look after your husband moved out with one of his twenty-
two-year-old math students. I wondered if Mrs. Lastrem had
shattered the picture frames, ripped the pictures in half, in
quarters, in eighths, then set them on fire in the backyard.
I drew my finger over the dust, smearing a line of dirt into
one of the white spaces.

"Don't," Polly said.

"What did she do with the pictures?"

"They're in a box."

"Where?"

"Under her bed, I think."

"Let's go look at them."

"No," Polly said, her voice high as she took a step back
from me. She looked confused, crinkling her nose and
squinting.

"Just kidding," I said, putting my hands in the air in front of me, like it was no big deal. The tip of my finger was dirty, and I wiped it on my pants while we went into her room. "You should wash your wall," I said, and Polly didn't say anything back.

We lay next to each other on the bed trying to study, Polly breathing through her nose, making a low whistling noise. The sound bothered me. I wanted to talk about her dad.

"Have you met her yet?" I said.

"No." She didn't look up from her book. It was geometry, columns of problems to be solved, pictures of rectangles and triangles with numbers along their edges.

"What if Mr. Stanley had an affair?" Our geometry teacher was bald and chinless. One of his pinkies was just a flap of skin and it jiggled in the air when he wrote on the board.

"Gross." Polly didn't look up.

"Would you have an affair with him?"

"Shut up."

"Are you going to meet her?"

"I don't know."

"Do you think she stays at his apartment with him?"

"I don't know."

"You don't want to talk about this, do you?"

Polly didn't say anything, kept staring at her book, the whistling sound getting louder. I knew she couldn't say no to me.

"Do you want to talk about it or not?" I said. Polly not being able to say no, it was part of what made me mean, made me forget to be careful with her. "Blow your nose," I said.

She opened her mouth to breathe, and the whistling stopped. The house was quiet around us. I could feel boredom washing over me in slow, lapping waves. We looked at our books a little while longer. I scanned the same sentences over and over, all the while trying to think of excuses to go home.

Kathleen invited me to a party at Jay Romano's. When I said, "Can I bring Polly?" she was quiet for a minute, and I wished I hadn't said anything, but then she said, "I guess." Polly said "No way" when I asked her, in a voice that made it sound like no one would want to go to a party at Jay Romano's, even though he was on the basketball team and two years older than us. At first, I was pissed at her, but then I was just relieved because I knew she'd have a bad time anyway.

I borrowed a short black skirt and a pink halter-top from Kathleen and tried putting my hair on top of my head like her mom's, but Kathleen said it looked stupid, so I wore it down.

After we had a couple beers, Tyler Silber took me into Jay Romano's bedroom. There was a floor-to-ceiling poster of Isaiah Thomas next to the bed. He wore his Pistons uniform and a sweatband, palming the basketball in a way that made the picture look 3-D, like he was going to throw the ball right to us. Isaiah Thomas' glossy brown eyes watched while Tyler Silber kissed me so hard, my teeth bit into the insides of my lips. Tyler's stubble rubbed against my cheeks while his hands moved quickly down my body, at my neck, then my tits, then between my legs. He took both of my wrists in one hand and held them over my head.

"Tyler," I said, and it came out like choking.

His mouth curled into a smile. There was something funny about the way he was looking at me, his eyes glazed and spacey. I was embarrassed of my armpits, my elbows, my knees. "What?" I said and his fingers moved inside me, quick and rough. I gasped, but it was soft, only a bit of air. Tyler closed his eyes; he was concentrating, biting his bottom lip, his head bobbing with the in out of his hand. The rhythm of his fingers was mindless, determined, achy.

I wanted to say, "What do you think of Mrs. Grange's buckteeth?" or "Do you know my name?" or "Tell me a secret," to get him to look at me, to laugh in my ear and whisper a joke. I tried to shift my weight beneath him, and he opened his eyes, staring at my neck and licking his lips. I wanted for a second to be him, to see what he was seeing.

"Tell me something," I said.

"Yeah," he said. Tyler Silber smelled of lemons. It was a good smell. It reminded me of soap.

Someone opened the door on us. There was a sudden burst of music and voices, but we couldn't see who stood there—a silhouette against the light—and my skirt was bunched around my waist, my underwear was down at my ankles, and Tyler Silber jumped on top of me so his body covered mine, and the person at the door yelled, "Fuck. Sorry," and laughed and closed the door, and Tyler Silber stayed on top of me like that for a second, and I liked how it felt, his body blanketing mine, and I hoped the person who opened the door had recognized my face, so they knew it was me back here with Tyler Silber.

I went to Polly's the next morning, my head still thick from beer. Her house was starting to change. Laundry sat in unwashed piles in front of the machine. Dirty dishes floated in a sink full of water. Mrs. Lastrem lay on the living room couch, her hair dark with grease and pressed flat against the side of her head.

"Hi, Mrs. Lastrem," I said.

She looked at me blankly, lifting her head and saying, "Hi Sara," before lying back down and closing her eyes. She used to be the pretty one, darker and thinner than her husband or daughter. When we were little, she would take us to the wave pool in the summertime, holding our hands while we jumped up and down in the water, screaming with us when we got splashed. Her bikini had a bright tropical pattern and sometimes when we jumped, her breasts crept out the top of the suit, the dark red curves of her nipples escaping the material. Whenever she laughed, the sound was loud and unashamed, and sometimes I'd fall against her on purpose, just so I could feel her wet skin on mine.

Polly sat in her room, still in her pajamas. "You missed a cool party," I said.

"You look bad. Were you drinking? Look at your eyes."

"Thanks, Mom. What did you do? Sit on your butt and watch TV?"

Polly didn't say anything. The air felt warm and heavy. They needed to open all the windows and run some fans in here; the house was going stale.

"I got together with Tyler Silber," I said. I was smiling.

"You're going to get a reputation."

I stared at Polly, her lips pursed together like an old lady.

There were things I wanted to tell her. How my crotch was sore and moist against my underwear, and I liked it. How I hadn't washed my hair yet and it smelled spicy and dirty like the two of us mixed together. How there were red teeth marks on my earlobe.

But I didn't say anything. Polly was shaking her head at me. I could already see her fading into the mess of this place. Reaching into the murky sink water to clean the dishes. Tiptoeing past her mother so she wouldn't wake her. Sitting silently on the mildewed couch in Leland Heights.

And up until then, I'd been feeling sorry for her, really bad about her whole situation, but when she said "You're going to get a reputation," I realized I was just tired of it and had been for a while now.

I started eating lunch with Kathleen. She wasn't someone I usually saw in school. Her friends smoked pot and shotgunned beers in their cars during lunch. But it was like she was just waiting for me to get sick of Polly because as soon as I asked her, she said yes, and then the next day she was there again as if this was how we'd always been doing it. Polly ate with us for a while, but it was like Kathleen and I were the real ones there and Polly was only the audience.

"Sally Tremaine has scabies," Kathleen said while she stirred the pasta on her tray. Steam rose from the noodles while she talked. "She got them from John Berke and he has herpes, too. I bet she'll get herpes soon."

"Sally Tremaine used to pick her nose," I said. "In the middle of class. She'd rub them on her pants or eat them when she thought no one was looking."

"What a skank!" Kathleen said.

Polly curled her nose like something smelled bad and stared at the far wall of the cafeteria.

"How was your history exam?" I asked her.

"Okay," she said.

In front of Kathleen, our conversations seemed stupid and small, so mostly I didn't talk to her.

We were standing at our lockers when Polly said, "You're going to eat with Kathleen all the time."

I looked away, into the mass of people moving through the hallway. They hurried by us, singly or huddled in small knots or yelling to each other in large, loose groups. Someone shouted "Bullshit!" and other people laughed. Two guys were shoving each other against lockers, making loud, crashing noises each time they bumped against the metal. A half-circle of people stopped to watch. I wanted to be there in the midst of it.

Polly made a noise, an impatient-sounding, "Huh?" Her eyes were wide and unblinking, her fists clenched at her sides. This was Polly trying to look determined, but it seemed more like an imitation of someone braver than herself. I stared as her chin began trembling, and something knife-sharp grew inside of me.

"Kathleen's my best friend," I said. For a moment, I was breathless, as if I'd been sucker-punched. My mouth tasted bitter and my throat grew warm.

Polly was silent. She swallowed hard, blinking quickly. Her fingers moved to her temple. Her lips started to shake. The bottom lip was wet and red, and it reminded me of a worm. I stood there watching it quiver and I didn't want to know her. I grabbed my books quickly, and when she called that night, I made my mother say I wasn't home.

She left notes. I knew they would come. Crammed into the grates of my locker, the paper misshapen to fit between the metal. *Remember how we used the Ouija board to find out you were going to have three kids? Remember pricking our fingers and rubbing the blood together?* I read parts aloud to Kathleen at lunch. One time she laughed so hard, chocolate milk came out of her nose. *What's the matter?* Polly always wrote at the end. *I'm sorry. I'm sorry. I'm sorry.*

She taped pictures to my locker, the two of us standing in our bathing suits at the beach, arms around each other, little girl bellies poking forward. Swinging on her jungle gym, my legs a blur from kicking. Fifth grade graduation. We wore handmade cardboard hats and wrinkled white gowns that only came to our knees. The four parents stood behind us, both of mine resting a hand on my shoulder, hers hugging each other. Polly and I smiled big, our lips tight from saying cheese for too long. She wrote *Remember?* in blue pen along the bottom, the word pressed so hard into the photograph, I could feel the letters with my fingers.

All of her attempts, they only made me bolder and more determined. I had been friends with Polly since we were seven. In fourth grade, I kicked Ryan Shepherd in the knee for calling her fat. The next year, I challenged two girls to a fight after they knocked Polly's books out of her hands. All through middle school, I told people to shut up when they teased her in the locker room. Loving someone, I realized, could make you a fool, blind to how sluggish and desperate and dull a person might be. But looking at Polly now, I saw. I was not going back. I was no fool.

She called. And called and called. Two, three, four times a night. I would never answer the phone. My parents retrieved messages off the machine when they got home from work, Polly's voice wild with emotion at times, a dull monotone at others. If they answered the phone, I would refuse the receiver when they handed it to me. At first, they gave tentative excuses—"She's asleep." "She's not here right now."—until finally giving up and saying, "Polly, she doesn't want to talk." They spoke in low, hurried tones afterwards and I listened through my door, satisfied by the frenzy of event, the odd chord of emotion in my mother's voice.

She knocked on my door one night. Polly had called twice already. It was a Friday and Kathleen and I were going to steal beer out of her fridge and take it to the park where the boys played basketball. I was curling my hair in my mirror. "Sara?"

my mother said, and it was funny to hear my name from her. Funny to then realize how rarely she spoke it.

She stood in the doorway. "This commotion with Polly has got to stop."

I looked at her through the mirror. She picked at her fingernails while she spoke, looking up briefly to meet my eyes in the glass.

"What commotion?"

"You need to talk to her."

"No, I don't."

"Young lady–" Her voice rose then wavered before she continued. "You are affecting this entire household with your behavior."

"Am I?" I watched my lips as I talked, full and pink. Jay Romano and Tyler Silber would be there tonight. The tops of my breasts curved just slightly over the neckline of my tank top.

"Yes, you are."

"No, I'm not."

My mother looked confused, the lines in her forehead deepening. Her mouth was half open, but she did not speak. We had never been here before.

"Sara–" she finally said.

"What?" I was loud and suddenly brave. "What do you want?" I watched my breasts move as I spoke, tiny jiggles.

"Sara, what's gotten into you?" Color rose in my mother's cheeks.

"What's gotten into *you*?" It was easy, this easy, to make noise. I had never known. "What the fuck?" I said.

A breath of air came out of my mother's mouth, a noise like a squeak, like someone getting hurt.

I watched myself in the mirror. I was large, large as a building, as a constellation. I was a superhero. A super villain.

Kathleen and I were at the mall when we saw Mr. Lastrem and his girlfriend. She was skinnier than I'd imagined. Her hair wasn't styled, just straight and long and brown and hanging down the sides, over her ears and far past her shoulders. She wasn't wearing any makeup and had lots of freckles. I could see her bra through her thin flowered shirt.

"That's Polly's dad," I told Kathleen when they were still a few stores away.

She put her hand over her mouth, pressing so hard, her laugh sounded like a fart. Everything had to be so dramatic with Kathleen. I ignored her. It felt like a long time ago when we were all sitting in Polly's car at the community college.

Mr. Lastrem stopped when he saw us.

"Hello, Sara," he said, and his mustache had grown so far over his top lip, he looked like a walrus. He and his girlfriend held hands and hers was like a doll's in his thick, stubby fingers. "How are you?"

"Fine, Mr. Lastrem," I said. The girlfriend was shifting on her heels, staring at me and Kathleen through heavy eyelids.

"This is Angela," he said.

Angela said *Hi* and let go of Mr. Lastrem, offering her hand to us. Kathleen shook first, looking Angela up and down, making a clucking sound with her tongue, before saying, "I'm Kathleen."

When I shook the girl's hand, it was bony and cool, and it seemed like if I pressed too hard, I could crush it. "Sara," I said.

Angela smiled at me, and her front two teeth were a little crooked, pointing in on themselves and making a V.

I was going to say, "I was friends with his daughter."

When I let go, she took Mr. Lastrem's hand again, and I noticed how her fingers pressed tightly against his and how she shifted her weight, bending a knee and rolling her foot onto its side so her body was tilted as close to his as possible.

Instantly, I could see it all. In his classroom, the first time his eyes lingered on her face too long after she'd answered a question. The day she felt his breath on her neck as he leaned over her desk, pointing out an inconsequential detail from her homework. When he asked her to come to his office because there was some information he needed to clarify. The moment he closed the door and put his hand on her shoulder, just a quick passing touch. She saw the ring on his finger, the photo of Polly and Mrs. Lastrem on his desk. She knew the destruction that lay before her. And she liked it, knowing for certain, for the first time in her life, she wasn't just some little girl. He moved his fingers along her cheek. Over her lips. She was a force to be reckoned with. He moved over her thin shirt to her breasts. She did not stop him. There were lives in her hands. She could change the world. He slipped his tongue in her mouth. She was happy.

carker

CONFERENCES WENT something like this: Jonna would wait in the front of her empty classroom, shifting from foot to foot like a show pony, resenting her dress suit. The wool would be pilled and too warm, the color an improbable green, the suit bought on the suggestion of a wide-hipped, yeasty colleague. *A suit*, Mrs. Ostrem had stage-whispered in the teacher's lounge, *will age you a little*. Parents like teachers with some life behind them. Mrs. Ostrem had been teaching social studies at Brookswood High for nineteen years, and her breath was sour with coffee, her hair falling out of its bun in long, thick strands, as if she'd just been shaken too hard.

Jonna would check the back of the suit regularly for chalk marks. She would try not to lean against her board. She would look out the window, though the classroom was like a cave at night—even more depressing than during the day, its puckered cinder-block walls reflecting back on themselves in the dark glass. Even this late into winter, nearly March, she would still feel affronted by the early arrival of nighttime, as if she were being cheated by the way the day's gray sky went black by five-thirty or six. She would stare at her reflection and think her face looked Munch-like and gaunt. She would check her breath in her palm.

She would listen to the voices and footsteps in the hallway. She would brace herself. If the noises faded, marching onward past her room, she would let her shoulders relax. If the noises grew louder and someone peered in, speaking her name—*Mrs. Lorre?*—she would fight the urge to say, *Two doors down.* She would smile as she corrected the *Mrs.* to *Ms.*

She would prefer the parents full of nervous fidgeting or the ones who couldn't make eye contact to the ones who brayed about their child's long-ago second-place finish in a fourth-grade spelling bee, or the ones who referred to each other (*Honey, Doll, Bar-Bar*) or their kid (*Stevie, Benj, Our Gal*) with pet names.

She would try to explain the course, Business Level English, without saying, *It's for the dumb kids.* The process reminded her of a game she once played drunkenly in grad school when she had to describe Mickey Mouse without saying Mickey or Mouse or Disney or cartoon or ears.

She would be interrogated. *Why did Frankie get a C- on his last paper? Why so many pop quizzes?* She would try to sound authoritative, using phrases like *striving toward performance benchmarks* and *creating an environment of learning and respect.* She would not reveal that this was her first job out of grad school; nor that she'd learned to bring a second blouse with her in the mornings, as she quickly pitted out the first one by the start of third period; nor that she had moved two thousand miles from home, lulled to the West Coast by Portland's cute public art and color-coded bus system; nor that she still barely knew her way around the gridded city; nor that she spent most of her time inert in her apartment, putting off trips even to the laundromat or the grocery store, wearing soiled stockings beneath her shoes and eating stale corn tortillas for breakfast; nor that she had only one friend here, a pug-nosed guy in the next apartment who wore tiresomely ironic T-shirts emblazoned with the names of landfills and nuclear power plants. She would clear her throat a lot.

Parents would grow angry, listing excuses for their children's poor performance and behavior: Lannie has ADD; Jessie's father and I are going through a divorce; Belle always struggles in the springtime. They would make diffuse accusations: Vince needs a certain sort of patience from his teachers; we just talked to Lucy's algebra teacher, and she's doing fine in there. Jonna would try not to twitch. Her left eye was known to twitch under stress.

Everyone would shake hands at the end—all except the angriest, who might walk out without so much as a goodbye. Jonna would usher the rest back into the hallway—ladies in their creased slacks, men with their ties loosed from their collars—and feel slightly bruised and naked, even after the least contentious interactions. She would watch their steady retreat—a husband lightly placing his hand on the back of a wife's neck; a single woman rifling through her purse for her car keys—and feel a slick, fleshy panic. The doorknob—she would hang on to it as the parents rounded the corner of the hall, out of view—would grow warm and damp in her grip.

Wait, she would think each time, even with the surliest or most belligerent of the bunch, who now seemed so full of purpose as they headed back to their lives beyond these walls. *Where are you going?* she would want to know with the urgent injustice of a child left with the babysitter. *Take me with you.*

All night, she'd been waiting for the Carkers. They were the seventh name on her list. She'd gotten through a weeping grandmother, two pissed-off dads, and three impatient couples. When they finally arrived, Mr. Carker turned out to be a bull-faced man, which didn't surprise Jonna. Mr. Carker's son was also bull-faced, with the same flat nose and wide nostrils, the same upper lip that seemed just short of a cleft palate—rising sharply at its midpoint and leaving the two front teeth partially exposed, even with a closed mouth. Just that—the insufficient coverage by the upper lip—left both father and son with a permanent expression of witless defiance.

Mr. Carker now paced slowly around the perimeter of Jonna's classroom, studying her Banned Books bulletin board, shaking his head in front of the index card about *The Adventures of Huckleberry Finn*. Jonna didn't know if this indicated his dislike of censorship or his dislike of her board. She clapped her hands softly to indicate it was time to begin; he ignored her.

Mrs. Carker was already sitting obediently at a student desk, playing with the program that had been handed out at the entrance of the school, rolling the corner of the bright green paper between her thumb and pointer finger. A full third of it was curled into a loose spiral. Jonna felt heartened by the inelegant curl; the same nervous tics that drove her mad with her students became suddenly reassuring when they came from the parents. I could take her, thought Jonna, as she assessed the woman's simple, cream-colored sweater and the noncommittal shimmer of her nail polish.

At the Current Events bulletin board, Mr. Carker fingered the famous picture of the president standing on the deck of an aircraft carrier in a flight suit. The paper wilted against its staples, the edges bowed forward from the thick heat of the school's old radiator system. "You talk politics in here?" he said. His voice was too loud for such a small room.

"No," Jonna said. "Well, yes. A lot of the reading we do is from magazines. Or newspapers."

"It's an English class. Not social studies," Mr. Carker said, still yelling. "When I was in high school, we read—" He paused for a moment. "Well, Dickens. I'm sure we read Dickens. And Kafka. The cockroach." He held his fingers in a claw, an apparent puppet of Gregor Samsa. Jonna tried to picture her class reading a book, these kids who sounded out words (and often incorrectly: *nostal-GUH, CHAY-os*), who carved up their desktops with nail files and cafeteria forks, who aspired to be NFL players or Navy Seals or, most commonly, nothing at all.

She gave him her speech on student anxiety about reading and how using nontraditional texts can lessen that anxiety. She was smiling as she talked. She sounded—even to her own ears—like a flight attendant or a salesgirl, someone whose job hinged on appeasement.

"Leonard likes current events?" Mr. Carker said as he fit himself into the student desk next to his wife, with the sort of unblinking eye contact that wavered between friendly and aggressive.

How strange to hear the boy called Leonard. Jonna had scarcely called him that since taking roll the first day, the rest of the class cackling and braying at the name. She hated the first day of the term, the way she was even less privy than usual to the in-jokes and elaborate sets of rules that seemed to knit together the chaotic, cruel fabric of high school. The first day was like being snow-blind, pushing forward stubbornly and stupidly, unable to see even the outlines of a path. Carker, they all called him—a rough, barking name for the boy with the uneven haircut and strange mouth who sat in the back corner of the room, the last desk next to the window, staring straight ahead, erect in his chair like a soldier.

"Leonard," she told the Carkers now, "is inconsistent with current events. He is, overall, an inconsistent student. I'm having some problems with him." She'd been formulating this speech for weeks, and she searched for signs of recognition in their faces, any indication that they'd heard this before. But Mrs. Carker was unreadable. She had the sleepy sort of eyes that made her look dumbly affable or bored or both. Mr. Carker squinted at Jonna through thin slits.

"Listen," Jonna said, her voice rising suddenly and unevenly. The crackle of that one word—such an immature, adolescent noise—rendered her speechless and filled her with a rush of familiar feeling: that of losing her footing, of stumbling surely and clumsily away from the neatly ordered thoughts of moments ago.

She had, by now, come to expect bad students. The incidents that had sent her home crying six months earlier—the boy ripping up a midterm exam in front of her; the girl throwing her puck-like pencil eraser at Jonna's face when Jonna insisted the girl stand and read aloud; the chalk rendition that appeared on her board one day after lunch, with two watermelon-like orbs for breasts, a patch of white curlicues for pubic hair, and a sign atop saying, simply, *Bitch*—now made her feel only numb and slightly queasy. At worst, she would maybe pick through her dinner, unable to eat, but she fell asleep soundly even after the days when phlegmy spit dripped from her classroom doorknob, or two boys passed what appeared to be a liquor bottle across the back row.

She'd come to understand these kids. They were bad because they were stupid. She'd learned about this in grad school: disruption due to discomfort in a standardized environment.

The boy who ripped up his midterm had not even the most basic comprehension of a sentence, let alone a paragraph; whenever the girl with the eraser spoke, she tripped herself up in a painful riddle of tics and stutters. They knew on some fundamental level that they were inadequate, and the misbehavior was their clumsy, groping effort to attract attention away from that. Their ineffective attempt at misdirection. On most days Jonna felt as if she were standing in front of a room full of shitty magicians, none of whom had mastered sleight of hand.

Carker, though, was different. Carker unnerved her. He was quiet and unusually self-possessed. He had good posture. Rather than slouching with the listlessness of most of his classmates, Carker sat erect in his seat, as if a ruler measured his spine. In the beginning, Jonna had mistaken this for alertness, homing in on the boy the way she often did with the one or two students who might offset the apathy of an entire class. But the first time she asked him a question—*What do you think is this author's central argument?*—after they'd read a short editorial opposing a state sales tax, Carker simply stared at her. His hands were clasped on his desk, the photocopy of the editorial centered neatly in front of him. "Leonard?" she said, after a moment had passed without a response. "Carker?" she tried. He continued to look at her as if she were an animal in a zoo and not a particularly exotic one, maybe a goose or a ferret, something that asked for his attention but failed to interest him.

The class had shifted and giggled as Jonna stood in front of the room, and Carker sat in the back, both silent now, staring at each other. Several students turned to look at Carker, but if he noticed, he gave no indication; his expression was as close to blank as one's could get while still awake, his features loose and impassive. Heat rose through Jonna's chest. She had grown familiar with the blustery hatching and scheming of her students, their fart noises and loudly dropped books. Quiet indifference unsettled her. "Carker?" she said one more time. Finally, he made a hissing noise, a low, wet sound between his teeth, as if he were declaring this standoff over, himself the winner. More giggles followed. Jonna eventually called on someone else, continued with her lesson, but for the rest of that day she couldn't get the image of the boy out of her head. Each time she flashed on him, the heat returned, as if she were revisiting a deep humiliation. Carker's empty face and his sly, snaky noise held an unnamed challenge; she felt somehow found out, revealed.

For weeks after that she watched the boy, looking for even the slightest bobble in his veneer—a brow furrowed in thought, a nod of recognition, even a disgusted scowl. But his face never changed; it held the same seemingly alert yet empty expression day in, day out. She made it a point to stand in the doorway at the start of his particular class period, greeting each student (*Nice to see you again, Tracy. Don't you look awake today, Lawrence?*), some of whom said a tepid hello back, while others squinted skeptically or laughed in embarrassment. *Top of the morning to you*, she'd said once to Carker, inexplicably; it was the first corny phrase to pop into her head. He ignored her, walking past without pause.

Any time Jonna called on him, they had the same mute standoff. "Carker? Carker?" she would call, as if beckoning a lost dog. Each time, Carker sat and stared. The rest of the class laughed or made dramatic displays of trying not to laugh, as if Jonna had accidentally said fuck (which she hadn't let slip since her third week) or left a middle button undone on her blouse, exposing her pink demi-bra (which she guarded vigilantly against, after one unfortunate morning near the end of fall term).

Each night, as she rode the bus home, she would try to shake off her day and regain the wonder of her first few weeks here, when she was awed by the greenness of this city compared to Detroit's rusts and grays, its dramatic sweep of bridges over the Willamette, its elevated light rail gliding through downtown's Pioneer Square. Everything had seemed so precious and well appointed, and she'd felt large within it, like a giant in a dollhouse of a city. It was exhilarating, existing in a place that had not yet been inhabited by her or any of the messy trails of her history. No one in Oregon knew that Seth Greenblatt had stood her up for the senior prom, or that her mother had once drunkenly called her a prissy bitch, or that she'd unwittingly bled through her green Capri pants on the third day of her trip across the country, discovering at a rest stop a stain that uncannily resembled the country of Spain and had left a deep pink imprint in her car's beige upholstery.

Now, though, when she cataloged the sites—the big pink building, the Made in Oregon sign, the purplish glow of the Hawthorne Bridge—they seemed already flat and disconnected from her, landmarks of someone else's city. She was on her way from the muggy, airless room where she worked to the muggy, airless room where she lived. These were the moments, as rain drizzled down the bus windows and the person in the aisle next to her talked importantly into his cellphone and the two girls in the seat in front of her giggled together, when she thought of Carker. She pictured his ugly mouth or ridiculous bangs, or she wondered what he was doing right then. He bled like this into her thoughts, trailing her unbidden through the lonely, soulless city.

"Leonard giving you problems?" Mr. Carker said, slouching awkwardly at his desk. Adults never fared well in these seats. They sat hemmed in by the desktop soldered to one of the metal arms. Mr. Carker kept repositioning himself to fit his knees beneath. Mrs. Carker swayed stiffly forward and back in hers, as if fearful of what she might catch were she to press too closely against any one surface. Jonna liked the gracelessness that the seats created, hoping it would keep the parents just uncomfortable enough to be docile.

"I can't tell what he's thinking," Jonna said. "He'll just sit there. Even when I call on him, he won't say anything."

Mrs. Carker said, "He can be quiet sometimes," with a voice as watery and thin as Jonna had imagined.

"It's more than that. I'm not really talking about quiet. He's pretty insolent," she said.

"Insolent?" Mr. Carker said slowly, as if he'd never heard the word before, let alone in conjunction with his son.

"Is he doing poorly?" Mrs. Carker stopped her swaying. Her husband rested his hand on her forearm, clasping it gently.

"It's not that simple," Jonna said. "He's a smart kid." In fact, she did not tell them, his writing revealed him to be uncommonly smart. While his sentences ran on from one to the next without even an attempt at punctuation, and his paragraphs were bloated and disorganized, his ideas were strong. In a stack of depthless papers about Afghanistan, while other students wrote thoughtlessly about terrorists and how bad it was for women to wear head scarves, Carker discussed the implications of U.S. funding of the mujahedin in the 1980s; in a paper about sex ed, while many classmates railed against how uncomfortable condoms were and how uptight parents could be, Carker asked how those who opposed contraception answered to the question of global overpopulation.

"But?" Mr. Carker said.

"But he's quietly disruptive," Jonna said.

"How can you be quiet and disruptive?" Mr. Carker said.

"By having a general air of defiance," Jonna said, clasping her hands in her lap. Her mouth felt dry. She wanted to cough or swallow but did neither.

Mr. Carker said quickly, "We've never had any problems with Leonard. He's a good kid. Gets his work done. Minds us." He leaned forward in the desk now, as if to show he could crawl over the top of it to get to her, need be.

"He's always gotten fine grades," Mrs. Carker added. "He passes every class." Her sleepy eyes were opened wider now, studying Jonna's face with an intent, unreadable expression. Was she issuing a challenge? A plea? She seemed to be sitting up straighter, gaining sudden confidence.

"I'm not talking about passing," Jonna said. "It's likely Leonard will pass. I'm talking about a bad attitude that is infecting the classroom."

"Leonard's infecting people?" Mrs. Carker said.

"Look," Mr. Carker said, in a tone that suggested he was going to put an end to this silliness, "Leonard's a good kid. He's had a paper route since he was eleven. He watches his sister every day after school. Real good with her. Doesn't just sit her down in front of the television. Reads to her. Books."

"You should see the way he talks to her," Mrs. Carker said. "He never teases her or pokes her. He talks to her just like she's his same age."

They were holding hands now, one of his and both of hers intertwined dramatically on his desk. "Used to be she had a hard time with the reading," Mr. Carker said. "But she's doing better now, since Leonard started with the books."

"That's nice," Jonna said dumbly. She was losing her momentum, as often happened in conferences, outmatched by the sheer, senseless force of parental love. With her grade book and detention slips, she was measly in comparison: a featherweight, half their age, with maybe a quarter of their conviction and loyalty.

She'd tried to avoid this altogether—the confrontation with the parents—by going directly to the boy instead. "Wait," she'd said to Carker one day, as his classmates filed out of the room. He backed himself against a wall, pressing into the concrete just next to the door, as if he hoped simply to slither out, unnoticed. From the hallway came rippling noises of students freed briefly and let loose upon each other, disparate shouts and the gleeful sort of laughter that often signaled a vicious bout of teasing. "I feel like there's some disconnect going on," she said. "Clearly you understand the material. But I'm not getting the sort of consistent participation I'd like to see. I don't think it's a learning issue. I think it's motivational."

Carker looked out the window. He seemed utterly at home in the gaping pauses of conversations. He stayed flat against that wall, even as the students from the next class began trickling in; he presented no resistance, no overt insolence, nothing Jonna felt she could point to clearly and punish.

"You're not presenting a problem," she stammered into his silence, "so much as a distinct lack. I think there's a lot more that you have to offer." Then, finally, more forcefully: "When I speak directly to you I expect a direct answer."

The students from the next class stared, open mouthed, a few grinning, as if they'd lucked onto a particularly violent car wreck.

"Okay," Carker said, but only, Jonna suspected, because he could sense that she was teetering on the edge of control. The word came out wispily, weightlessly, as if it were a cough or sigh, something that escaped his lips with little of his own volition.

And still nothing changed. The standoffs continued in class. The whole room quickened, grew altogether more alert and interested each time Jonna stood before them, trying to cajole Carker from his silence. She sensed, too, the other students beginning to be swayed by him. Classmates turned to gauge whether he had any response when Jonna announced a pop quiz or the due date of a writing assignment, as if he were the silent arbiter of classroom opinion. Sometimes, a wave of unaccountable snickering would ripple from his corner of the room. Jonna was never able to identify the source. As she surveyed the faces, most students fidgeted guiltily in their seats while Carker stared at her, empty.

If Jonna had had more self-control, she would have simply ignored him. But she found herself regularly checking his reaction as she lectured, her compass unaccountably drawn in his direction. It was like a tic she'd developed, glancing to the back right every few minutes. She was waiting for something, anything. But Carker remained utterly, improbably immobile. Little effort seemed required on his part, as if his stance were meditative, as if he'd successfully accomplished what they all longed for: wresting his mind from the physical shell that was forced into this desk fifty-five minutes a day. To each of Jonna's glances his way, his stillness seemed to be simply and unapologetically asking, *Who cares?* and *What does any of this matter?*

In graduate school, they'd talked about teaching as though they were training to be superheroes. Reaching the unreachable and empowering the disenfranchised. They talked about educational reform; they talked about multiculturalism; they talked about reframing the idea of learning disabilities into learning differences. Jonna received A's on everything. She student taught with an old, peach-faced woman who'd been teaching AP English forever and who regularly whipped her students into shouting frenzies over Ayn Rand's objectivism or George Orwell's prescience about the current government. Jonna prepared meticulous lesson plans about Hobbesian philosophy and *Lord of the Flies* or naturalism in *Ethan Frome*, and the students lapped it up, taking furious notes in their loose-leaf binders with each word Jonna spoke.

She'd thought of all this during her first-term performance review. Shel Dougan, Brookswood's principal, had sat her down a few weeks before conferences and mixed several metaphors, talking about learning to walk before she could run and getting her feet wet and steadying her sea legs. He told her not to feel bad about the comments veteran teachers had made after their classroom observations: *Ms. Lorre seems to have a tenuous grasp, at best, on classroom management strategies. Ms. Lorre appeared to have lost her train of thought more than once. Mrs. Lorre seems to be easily intimidated by student resistance to the material.*

Jonna had stared past the principal's balding head into the student parking lot beyond his picture window. There were dual-cab trucks and all-wheel-drive wagons, row after row of shiny SUVs. She wondered which one was Carker's.

"It's not cause to worry," said Shel Dougan, in a tone that indicated otherwise.

"Look," Jonna said, pointing to four kids snaking through the lot, hunching low with their sweatshirt hoods tied around their heads. It was third period. Shel Dougan turned to look as they filed quickly into a beat-up Jeep. When he turned back to Jonna he looked tired, but he was also smiling, as if the two of them were in on some sort of a joke. She wasn't sure what that joke might be.

The car peeled out from the lot. Shel Dougan held his hands up at his sides. "What can you do?" he said softly.

Carker's parents were getting anxious and impatient; Jonna could see as much. The mother chewed on her bottom lip, the father tapped his foot loudly against the floor tiles.

"Tell me," Jonna said now, changing tactics. "What has Leonard told you about the class?"

Mrs. Carker shook her head. Mr. Carker shrugged. "Nothing," he said simply.

"We don't hear much," his wife added.

"Oh. Okay. All right," Jonna said, feeling a warm rush of disappointment. It was hard to imagine that he'd said nothing, not even a brief mention, a casual complaint or snide remark. She was flushed now, caught in the quiet embarrassment of the unrequited.

"I'm sure there's been some sort of misunderstanding," Mrs. Carker said, her voice steadily gaining strength. "Leonard would never be purposefully disrespectful."

"Damn right," Mr. Carker said—and then, quickly, "Pardon my French." He started in on a meandering story about a time in Boy Scouts when Carker helped some kids build a tent in the rain.

Jonna wasn't sure what to say. She'd hoped they'd be apologetic and complicit, worn down from years of disappointment and heartbreak. Their child, after all, was in Business Level English. Such a thing did not happen by accident, but after nearly continuous missteps and fuckups. She thought of her own parents; she did not often think of them, but conferences forced the issue, confronting her with hours of parents not her own. Jonna found it hard to imagine them like this: panicked and desperately defensive. The last contact she'd had was months ago when she'd called—frantic, unthinking—because she'd been unable to disarm a smoke alarm in her apartment, even after having doused the burnt pot of rice, yanked the alarm from the ceiling, and searched impotently for a battery compartment.

When her mother answered, her voice was slurred by gin. "Sweetheart," she called Jonna, and "Doll." Her father shouted at her to rip out the battery and wouldn't concede when she insisted there was no compartment. He told her to stop being pig-headed and listen to him. She told him she was listening. The noise of the alarm was a piercing bleat. He told her to rip the goddamn battery out. She said there was no battery compartment. He swore some more. She hung up and smashed the alarm with a hammer, gouging several deep divots in her already pocked hardwood floor.

Mr. Carker's story ended with his son saving a few other kids from catching pneumonia. He leaned forward again, looking smug and satisfied, as if he'd just made an unassailable point. "How long have you been at this?" he said. "We almost walked right past your room at first; we didn't realize you were the teacher." He was smiling, but Jonna heard the challenge in his voice.

Her cheeks grew warm. The wool of the suit was itchy on her arms through her thin blouse. "Long enough," she said. There was the slightest quaver to her voice, and she hated herself for it. Mr. Carker stared at her. She held his gaze for one beat, then another, finally looking past him to his son's desk—because that's what it had become, Carker's desk, even when it was empty.

She flashed on the class two Tuesdays ago when they'd been discussing an article claiming high school kids were being over-diagnosed with ADHD. Jonna thought the topic would be popular, given how many of her students faithfully visited the school nurse to receive their Ritalin or Adderall or Dexedrine. But they sat square jawed and yawning, doodling in their notebooks, resting their heads heavily in their hands.

"If this author visited Brookswood, would the visit confirm or challenge his opinion?" Jonna asked. She was in front of her desk, leaning against its edge, somewhere between sitting and standing, her hands clasped loosely at her waist. This was the pose she remembered from her own English teachers, one of friendly, casual confidence, as if they'd all just gathered here to chat. Bryn Martin cracked her gum loudly in the front row. Justin Scott kicked at the floor, his gym shoes making short, sharp squeaks against the tiles. Carker sat in the back, blankly watching her.

"Anyone?" Jonna said. "Lorraine?"

Lorraine Ingram—greasy hair, third row—looked up from her desk, blinking quickly, as if Jonna had just slapped her. "I don't know. Confirm?"

"Why do you say confirm?"

Lorraine shrugged. She sat for a long time, as if she were thinking. "I don't know. Challenge?"

"Why challenge?" Jonna said, trying to keep her voice even and well-modulated.

"What was the question again?" the girl said.

"Dumbass," Roger LeBron whispered from the next row.

"And what's your opinion on this, Roger?" Jonna said quickly.

"Lots of people I know doped up on speed," he said. He had the craggy, asymmetrical face of someone who'd been beaten up a lot.

"And what do you make of that?" Teaching, Jonna had discovered, was mostly weaving together flimsy filaments of thought and then acting as though the result created something of substance.

"Don't make anything of it," Roger said.

"Does anyone make anything of that?" she called out, watching the roomful of eyes watching her. The wall heater made its rhythmic ticking noise; the air felt thick and unwashed. She could taste the yellow flecks of chalk in the back of her throat, feel them on her fingertips and in her hair. That soft yellow powder was pervasive, inescapable. Jonna found it on the seat of her car, the faucet in her bathroom at home, her pillowcases and sheets—the shadow of this room following her everywhere.

"Anyone?" she repeated. "How about Sam?" she finally said. "Sam, what do you think?"

She had come to rely on Sam Larimer—and a few other students like him—in this way, as a rescue. He was a stick-thin, zit-faced, hardworking kid who ran his finger beneath the lines of words as he read aloud, cleared his throat incessantly, and pressed so hard when he wrote that he often broke off the tips of his pencils and had to use the sharpener over and over again. These quirks—along with a history of related quirks, Jonna suspected—left Sam open to merciless teasing. Each time he went to the sharpener, he was pelted with spitballs. *Pencil dick*, they called him. The mocking only seemed to worsen if Jonna yelled at them to stop, as if she were trying to discourage a swarm of bees by swatting at them. So she watched impotently as Sam got torn to bits, and she tried to make up for it by writing encouraging notes on his essays and frequently soliciting his opinions, which he always framed proudly in stiff, bookish terms: "Well, it appears patently obvious to me that…" or "I am of the mind that…" He only lost his train of thought occasionally, as classmates coughed loud insults into their fists.

"Sam, do you think kids are being overdiagnosed with disorders?" she asked him now. He was good for deflecting attention away from Jonna, if only because he was the one person in the room less liked than she was.

Sam began to open his mouth, then suddenly stopped. His eyes darted in one direction, then another; his hands fluttered quickly in his lap. He took a deep breath and came to a strange sort of halt, sitting almost still, staring at Jonna. His face was nervous, though, the corner of his lip pulsing like a heartbeat.

"Sam?" Jonna said.

The boy continued to stare at her. He sealed his lips tightly together, as if in a dramatic display of buttoning it. For a moment, Jonna was confused; she continued to repeat his name, and he continued to sit. Someone began chuckling, and another few students let out low whooping noises. Roger LeBron called out, "Sammy!" in a tone far less mocking than usual. Jonna was only one beat slower than the rest of them in realizing what was happening. Sam sat up straighter in his chair now, shifting his narrow shoulders back, staring straight ahead as the hum of noise grew around him. He was, she saw now, trying to pull a Carker. His lips were still pressed tightly together, but now they suppressed a grin. Jonna felt a hot, thick anger and a desire to slap the kid across his zitty red cheek. He'd sold her out.

She looked involuntarily to the back corner by the window, and there Carker sat, his mouth also spread thinly across his face in the tiniest little smile. The expression was odd, almost creepy. She'd never seen Carker smile before.

"Leonard …" Her voice was shaky, but loud. "What is your opinion on this?" She couldn't even remember her original question. She marched toward the back of the classroom, toward his desk. "What do you have to say about it all?" She was yelling. Carker stared at her, with the same bemused expression. She stood right next to his desk, watching the slow, even rise and fall of his striped T-shirt.

"Leonard! Why don't you grace the class with your opinion? Care to open your mouth, or would you prefer to sit back here on high?" She was spitting. The wet spray flew through the air, some landing on Carker's desk, some glistening on his cheek. He didn't wipe it away. The room was silent. Jonna didn't know if she'd ever heard it so quiet. "You think you could do better?" she yelled, waving toward the front of the classroom. She knew she was acting crazily, but she felt a light, buzzy sensation in her chest, as if she were coming up for breath after a long time submerged. "You think you can do better than me, Leonard?" she yelled. "Go for it!" She was standing so close, she could smell his fishy mouth from the cafeteria lunch. He had something pale and fleshy caught between his front two teeth. "Go for it!" she yelled, and for a moment there was nothing, just quiet all around her.

Jonna made a sudden starting motion, as if she might head-butt Carker, and he flinched. She was deeply satisfied by that. She hung there, inches from his face, as his smile faded. Carker had a scrawny little chest, Jonna realized. He also had a light patch of freckles beneath his left eye. She fought to hold her pose; there was, she deduced, no going back from this. Her breath was coming through her nostrils in a forceful rush. A slight tingling had begun to travel up the back of her neck, from the strange angle of it. She was about to buck forward again, to see if he would flinch again—it was the only thing she could think of—when the boy finally, thankfully, raised both arms in the air as if in surrender.

Carker stood up slowly from his desk and slipped past her, his face bright and full of color. Carker walked to the front of the room—it was more of a shuffle, his feet sliding heavily against the floor, his hands tucked in his pockets, his head bent forward. He looked suddenly different than usual—younger, his shoulder blades poking through the back of his shirt like a pair of parentheses. Jonna felt a quick flash of uncertainty. She eased into the empty desk next to Carker's, Liz Lopshire's; she was an unfortunate girl often absent due to a bleak cocktail of asthma and allergies. When Carker got to the front of the room, he slouched against her desk. He was all curves now—the slope of his back, the bend of his neck, and his loose, liquid arms—a pale imitation of his normal ramrod self.

"Go ahead!" Jonna yelled. The boy moved his lips, as if he was going to say something, but no sound came out.

The rest of the class was caught between excitement and confusion, some kids leaning forward in their seats to gawk at Carker, others twisting around to look at Jonna, most shifting between the two, forward and back, trying to take in the whole situation. A rippling anticipation moved through the seats. Wordless noises came from the crowd—a cawing laugh, a low, grunting, question-like sound. But no one said anything. Everyone was waiting.

Finally, Carker ran his fingers once through his uneven haircut and said, "How many of you are on drugs?" His voice was low but surprisingly uneven, the last word coming out in a breathy squeak.

The class laughed.

"Prescription drugs?" Carker said quickly, his face reddening more deeply.

Hands went up.

"Donovan," Carker said, pointing to one. "What're you on?"

The boy listed several drugs, his voice crackling. Donovan Barrett had barely spoken all term. Carker's voice grew a little louder as he asked, "How many of you have to talk to a shrink?" Hands went up. Leslie Torneau talked about a therapist who recommended hospitalization when she was eleven. Carker nodded. "How old were you when you first saw a shrink?" he asked, and "Who wanted you to go, you or your parents? Do the drugs even make you feel better?" Mike Johannsen said he crushed up his slow-release capsules for a better buzz. Barrett Glenn once stole a few of his mom's Valium, which helped him relax and get his work done.

These weren't kids who normally talked. The air of conspiracy that usually thrummed just below the surface, between Carker and the rest of them, had been let loose. They were—all of them—giddy with sudden power.

Soon Carker began imitating Jonna. "What conclusion can we draw from that?" he said in a high-pitched voice—one of her standard lines. He never once looked her way. Other students, though, kept peering back, looking for her reaction, maybe waiting for her to put a stop to this and regain control. But she just sat, awash in this stifling room with its muddied floor tiles and fingerprint-stained windows and littered mess of papers and candy wrappers and pen caps underfoot.

"What you're telling me," Carker said from the front of the class, swooshing his arms through the air like a conductor, "is you're a bunch of addicts." Everyone laughed. Jonna could taste shame in her throat, hot and metallic. But beneath it lay something else, something pulsing and distinct: it was relief, the bright and certain relief of sitting back in the cheap seats, at just the slightest remove—six measly rows, but it felt like a chasm—from the pressure, the performance, the small, small life she'd so quickly amassed up there in front of these little animals.

Carker went on.

Mr. Carker was calling her *ma'am* now. Jonna was only half listening, gleaning a few pieces of sentences here and there. "I understand a room full of them must be a handful, ma'am… We've been pretty lucky with him, ma'am…"

His wife sat with the thinnest, stiffest smile, as if she'd been posing for a picture for several beats too long.

Jonna was sick to death of parents. Their love seemed valueless, devoid of any balance or scale, if even the rotten kids were swaddled protectively by it. She imagined the way Mrs. Carker tucked her son's hair behind his ear at the breakfast table and how Mr. Carker playfully punched him in the shoulder as they sparred about which baseball team would win the pennant this year. She wondered about the pet names they might have for him and what predictable pictures they had framed along the staircase—Carker as a naked baby, Carker in his Sunday best, Carker in his Little League uniform, Carker posed with his sister and parents in wicker chairs against a fake blue background in some downscale department store photo studio.

Jonna had, since two Tuesdays ago, successfully ignored Carker. Or at least successfully appeared to be ignoring him. She never called on him, never looked at him. But she felt him from his corner, like a lamp turned up too brightly, its bulb heating her face. And the rest of the class hadn't yet righted itself. Sam Larimer still refused to talk. Donovan Barrett was sent to the office after calling her an asshole. A half-dozen kids, in a strikingly premeditated act of disobedience, wrote *Don't know don't care* across the latest reading quiz.

There was a rapping at her door. Jonna saw the faces of the next parents through the chicken-wire window. She looked at her list and saw that they belonged to Debbie Trainor, who had prominent buck teeth and regularly forgot to write verbs into her sentences. Jonna had nine more sets of parents to meet after them. There was a deep throbbing at the base of her neck, as if it might simply snap from her shoulders, sending her head rolling across the mucky floor. She was not altogether put off by the image.

She held one finger up to the Trainors. Wait, please.

"Well," Mr. Carker said, disentangling himself from his desk. "We won't keep you." Mrs. Carker followed his lead, and Jonna had no other choice but to stand.

How long she'd been waiting to meet them. How sure she'd been that they—by their very existence—would provide answers about the boy. But now they stood inches away from her, Mr. Carker with a mole in front of his right ear, his face pale like winter, and Mrs. Carker with her unassuming middle-aged haircut, short, gray-flecked layers around the face with a blow-dried lift at the top. Neither of them offered her anything. And now they were trying to leave. Jonna felt twisted around and jarred loose, like at the abrupt moment of waking from a dream of free-fall.

"Wait," she said. Her voice sounded like a child's. "Please. Sit."

Mrs. Carker looked to her husband to take the lead. Jonna did the same. What was it, she wondered, with the fucking men in this family? Slowly, though, he sat, faintly shaking his head. His wife sat, too. Jonna remained standing.

For one long beat, then another, she stared at them, trying to collect herself. This isn't easy for me, she imagined beginning. But there was, she'd tell them, something seriously wrong with their son. Ser-i-ous-ly, she would repeat. He was antisocial to the point of being maladaptive. Or maybe she would say he shows no concern for the well-being of others. Or maybe both. He was malicious, mean-natured, and dangerous, she would tell them, punctuating each word with a gesture—a finger pointed directly at them or her hands clapping softly together. He had, she would continue, sociopathic tendencies. His intelligence, rather than being an asset, was hazardous to others. To the safety of others, she might emphasize, depending on their reactions. He was powerful and shouldn't be underestimated, she'd say, pausing to let the words sink in, but only for a brief moment—not long enough to let them begin a defense.

Their boy was sick, she would continue. She liked that word, sick. Maybe she'd repeat it. He needed some sort of intervention, she'd say—counseling or medication or a strong cocktail of the two. They should not delay. They should get help as soon as possible.

Here she would pause a final time, possibly walking behind her desk to lean her hands on it as she searched for the perfect metaphor. Leonard was, she'd say, a ticking bomb, an undetonated land mine, a sniper lying in wait.

The Carkers, she knew, would dismiss her claims, Mr. Carker likely yelling, Mrs. Carker crying. They'd storm out, maybe write her a nasty letter, complain to Shel Dougan and then to Dustin Lourdes, head of the school board. They'd go home and hold Carker tightly, pet his head, speak cooing, reassuring words into his ear. Maybe they'd finally buy him that PlayStation 2 or schedule that long-promised trip to

Disneyland. They would joke quietly with each other—safely out of the children's earshot—about what a nut that teacher had been. They'd spin their fingers next to their ears. *Cuckoo. Cuckoo.*

But the next time Carker pulled his sister's hair, the next time he broke curfew, the next time he sulked through dinner, they would wonder. They would feel a tiny sliver of doubt. Jonna would have planted the seed, would have begun to wrest him from them, them from him.

The Trainors knocked again on the door. Jonna held up her entire hand this time: *Stop.* They could wait their turn. The words—bitter, violent, sudden as vomit—were coming.

all that apply

THE FORM SAID *What is the nature of your workplace injury?* It said *Check all that apply*, which struck Em as so generous, she thought she might cry, though that had to be the painkillers. Em wasn't normally a crier, and she knew not to get emotional in front of the nurses, because then they'd slow down her painkillers to show that painkillers were the reward for patients who weren't pains in their asses.

- ☐ lifting (back)
- ☐ lifting (hernia)
- ☐ ladder (fall, sprain, or break)
- ☐ ladder (fall, concussion)
- ☐ heavy machinery (limb)
- ☐ heavy machinery (trunk)

Em's job involved no lifting, no ladder, no heavy machinery. She imagined a trunk injury–a man's torso as a gouged piece of luggage. Word play had been wonderful to her as a girl, a kind of magic. She'd been a dumb girl, though dumb in a good way or at least enviable now.

- ☐ vehicle (cuts/lacerations)

☐ vehicle (head trauma)
☐ vehicle (ejection)

Her job involved no vehicle. She pictured the man with luggage for a torso ejected from a car, landing on his head. She thought: I am amusing myself. She thought: barely.

☐ job site (fall)
☐ job site (falling object)
☐ job site (collision with person)
☐ job site (collision with vehicle)
☐ job site (collision with other)

Em didn't have a job site unless an office was a job site. Unless a desk. She read books and wrote summaries of the books and what she thought of the summarized books. Her employer told her to stop writing *I think* at the start of her sentences, though Em's job was to write what she thought. Her employer told her to stop writing *Dear Pamela* at the start of every email. She didn't need a salutation. This isn't Microsoft, her employer told her, which Em didn't know how to take. Microsoft had a campus. Microsoft fed employees in a slick cafeteria. Microsoft let people work from beanbag chairs in rumpus rooms. She either knew this about Microsoft or was making it up. She'd read it online maybe or read tweets from people who'd read it online.

☐ fall (ice)
☐ fall (staircase)
☐ fall (sidewalk)
☐ fall (job site)

Em wondered what the difference was between *job site (fall)* and *fall (job site)*. She wondered if the redundancy was carelessness or a trick. She would not be tricked. The one thing she was good at was reading. She read carefully, even if she didn't know how to write an email. Even if she was or was not fit to work for Microsoft. Also, she had not fallen.

At the bottom of the form:

☐   other: _____

The blank line was shorter than her pinkie finger. She didn't know how to fit spilling the cheap employee coffee on her hand and then remaining incredulous of the pain even after running and running it under cold water in the employee sink, incredulous still of the blisters, fascinated by them, poking and poking for days, first with her fingernail, then a tine of her dinner fork, then the needle she had for the irreverent cross-stitch (*ok, boomer*) she'd enthusiastically ordered from Etsy and then enthusiastically ignored, until the blisters popped one by one. The blisters oozed. (*Enough with the passive voice*, her employer told her in a salutationless email.)

Em had continued going to work because she could read one handed, she could write. The workplace injury (which she'd not thought of as a workplace injury yet, but rather one more unfortunate thing she'd done to herself and wished she could take back and could not take back and in lieu of any possibility of taking it back, adopted the belief that if she did absolutely nothing about it, it would go away) was to her non-dominant hand.

In bed at night, the pain kept her awake, and she wished for:

- ☐ antibiotic ointment
- ☐ Tylenol
- ☐ non-stick Band-Aids

though these would have involved getting out of bed and walking down eight flights of stairs and half a block to the bodega where the nighttime woman (cherry cheeks, enthusiastic English) knew her by sight, which sometimes warmed Em and sometimes made her egregiously lonely. Getting out of bed did not fit with her plan of doing absolutely nothing. Em was, if nothing else, a person who stuck to her plans. A plan was how she ended up in:

- ☐ a city with a subway
- ☐ an apartment like a closet
- ☐ atop a vertical quarter mile of stairs

At work, she tried to focus on the book she was reading for her employer because it was a good book and most of the books she read for her employer were bad. Children died but beautifully. Men made fools of themselves but heartbreakingly. The world was an apocalypse but hopefully.

"Stop with all the adv–" her employer came out of her office to say, except her employer didn't say, because her employer was standing close enough to see. "Oh my," her employer said, which may have been the first nice thing she had ever said to Em. "God." Em waited for her employer to tell her what to do. Em waited hopefully. "Get that," her employer said, "taken care of."

In bed at night, the pain made her wish:

- ☐ personal vehicle
- ☐ primary care doctor
- ☐ emergency contact

In bed at night, the pain:

- ☐ her stupid hometown
- ☐ its stupid McMansions
- ☐ its stupid parking lots for days

In bed at night:

- ☐ her narrow girlhood mattress
- ☐ thermometer under her tongue
- ☐ her (dead, post-boomer) mother's hand on her forehead
- ☐ "there, there"

She woke from never having fallen asleep to a meat thing where her hand used to be. She held the meat thing by the wrist and cried.

The Uber driver told her *Christ* and *What the hell?* I know, Em said, though she did not. Nothing ever having hurt this bad had made her believe nothing would ever hurt this bad. She didn't know coffee could do this. She didn't know blisters could do this. She made involuntary noises over potholes as quietly as possible:

- ☐ *guh*
- ☐ *aak*

The Uber driver asked her which hospital. Em didn't know which hospital. Em let the Uber driver pick.

☐ *fu–*
☐ *sss*

She loved the nurses, even the mean ones who lectured her. Ira was the meanest nurse's name, and Em said it every chance she could—*Hi Ira. Hello Ira*—because she was allowed salutations here, and what Ira was doing with the IV and ointment and the painkillers had turned the pain into something dull and faraway. Her employer left an angry voicemail. Em had forgotten to call in sick. Em told herself she would call and explain. Em told herself she would call and apologize.

Ira fed her pills in miniature plastic cups, followed by water in miniature plastic cups. She'd loved miniature anything as a girl: miniature dinner plate and miniature toilet paper roll and miniature potted plant, arranging and rearranging in her dollhouse. She told Ira *dollhouse* aware of being not herself or being more herself or contiguous to herself from the pain and then the cessation of pain and then the return of pain in smaller and smaller waves that no longer made her cry. She was always grateful to be not crying. She asked, *that's how a girl's supposed to picture a life, Ira?*

Ira did not answer. Ira delivered a lecture on wound care, a lecture on lucky you have medical insurance any idea how much this little stint was going to cost her, a lecture on a girl like you no reason to end up here, Em halfway sure she was falling in love with Ira, Ira thinking she was a girl like her even with her meat thing and her excessive salutations and her dollhouse dreams.

Ira was the one who gave her the form. She and Ira were having a fight in which Ira was correct on all counts and she was:

☐   other: _____

She'd always thought of herself as an *all that apply* but it turned out she was a *none of the above*. Okay. That was okay. If she looked long enough at the blank line, she could make it blur into a squiggle. If she stared and stared, she could make it start to whorl. She wondered if this was the painkillers, or the low overhead lighting, or something she'd always been able to do had she bothered, or something anyone could do. She hoped it wasn't something anyone could do. She hoped she was special, though being special inside her own eyeballs was less than ideal. She'd have to explain for anyone to notice. She'd have to tell Ira: *Ira, look what I can do.*

congratulations, baby

"JANE LOOKS LIKE A BLIMP," Moira says to me in Jane's kitchen. Moira's leaning on the beige counter-topped island, and I'm backed against the fridge. I can feel the hum of it against my shoulder blades, and the low vibration's vaguely soothing. The women in the living room laugh in a shrill, hyena-like way. It sounds rehearsed, the way their voices keep peaking and then lulling together. Moira's drinking a Tom Collins, and she's spread Jane's sugar bowl, ice cube tray, and bottles of gin and club soda along the countertop. She's been doing this all afternoon, refreshing her Tom Collins and ushering me into the kitchen so she can say mean things about Jane. Moira was the girl who dared each of us to get naked as teenagers, so we could rate each other's bodies. That's cellulite, she said to me one time, shaking a finger at my bare ass.

There are a bunch of pots and pans hanging upside down from the ceiling over her head. For a second, I have a fantasy of one of them coming down on her skull and leaving a sprouting red lump, a ring of stars circling round. They are substantial pieces of kitchenware, hefty silver handles and thick bodies, All-Clad stamped on the sides. Jane used to have an efficiency with fly strips hanging dirtied and tangled from the ceiling; the only knives she owned were the serrated ones we pocketed each time we went to the Red Lobster.

"Well she certainly isn't skinny," I say.

Moira laughs an open-mouthed laugh, holding her belly, like what I said is far funnier than what I've said. "That's for damn sure," she says, wiping the back of her hand against her eyes, as if she's wiping away tears of joy. "And what's up with the outfits?" she goes on, pointing a thumb to the living room. "Does being a mother mean you have to forsake all style?"

Moira has had two abortions. She was twenty-four when she had the last one, six years ago, and I was the one who drove her to Planned Parenthood. She held my hand in the waiting room, her face spongy and moist. On the ride home, she asked if it was okay for her to sit in the back and then she crawled in like a dog and curled up along the length of the seat. "Seatbelt," I said because I couldn't think of anything else, but she ignored me. I had shitty shock absorbers in that car and whenever we went over potholes, her whole body flopped against the seat. She didn't call me for weeks afterwards, even after I left messages, as if the whole thing had been somehow my fault.

She cracks the ice tray now and drops the cubes into the soda, and they make a loud, fizzy noise. Her eyes are raccoony, with their dark circles; tiny red spider veins snake along her cheeks. "You want?" She holds up her glass. I shake my head. Drinking makes me feel old and tired and, besides, Moira's the only one having anything other than the non-alcoholic fruit punch that Jane's neighbor, Nadine, brought over in a big plastic bowl.

"Jane's dressed like the fucking grand ol' flag," Moira says. It's tempting to fall into this banter. Moira and I are well-practiced; Jane's been an easy target ever since she picked out the wedding dress with the hoop skirt and the petticoats. She lives in the suburbs, she works happily behind a neat desk at a bank, she talks about her deep love for her husband without even the slightest hint of irony. But I'm not in the mood today, not in this house full of strangers.

"Come on," I say, heading back to the living room.

Moira grabs my arm as I walk past. "If I have to hear one more story about burping or feeding or baby puke, I'm going to slit my goddamned wrists." She holds her wrist to my face for emphasis. Moira needs to make her unhappiness communicable, incapable of being miserable quietly or alone.

"Let go," I say.

"Oh, am I holding B.B. back from honorary membership in the suburban mom club?" Moira says. Her breath is sweet and hot with gin. "I'm so sorry. Go have your fun." She lets go of my arm, and stares at me slack-mouthed with her head cocked to the side, like she's ready to fight. It's so easy to veer into this place with Moira, one misstep and you've crossed the line into her hurt or anger or bottomless something-or-other. My friendship with her is viral. There is no treatment; you just have to ride it out. When I head for the living room, she's right behind me, her breath loud and forceful.

The women are sitting in a wide circle, talking about family beds. "Darren's worried about putting the baby in the bedroom with us," Jane says, giving me and Moira a quick, appraising glance as we sit. She's in the recliner, her legs spread and her hands cupping the bottom of her huge belly. Blimp isn't the right word. Jane was never skinny; she had the biggest tits of any of us in high school, but they weren't revered like cheerleader tits or homecoming queen tits because she had wide hips and thick thighs too. But Jane wasn't a fat girl.

She fell somewhere in between, wearing long T-shirts with jeans or loose cottony dresses, but then spicing it up with her red cowboy boots or silver disco belt or studded neck collar. People never messed with Jane. She was one of those plain girls who believed her parents when they told her she was beautiful.

She's wearing a blue-and-white polka-dotted maternity shirt and red stretchy pants today. Jane looks good pregnant—the round face and thick fingers and ruddy cheeks suit her. The way she's sprawled in the recliner, rubbing her belly, it's like she's holding court.

"He thinks we'll never have sex if the baby's in the bed," she says.

"You'll never have sex regardless," Sandy, one of Jane's co-workers, says from the couch. Everyone laughs; the women's mouths are red from the punch, the edges of their lips and tongues a bright surprise. I laugh too, but my voice sounds shrill and fake. Moira is humming next to me, a low, impatient sound.

"I'd just be afraid I'd roll right over and crush the little thing," Wendy, the other co-worker on the couch, says. Sandy and Wendy both have layered haircuts with a heavy emphasis on the bangs, and both are wearing elaborate sweaters; Sandy's is red and black with silhouettes of those little Scottish terriers. Wendy's is a tan and green argyle that reminds me of the socks that Jane, Moira and I wore fanatically and competitively for several seasons.

Nadine, the next-door neighbor, says: "Jed and Brian slept in their own rooms, but I finally gave in with Alexis." Nadine's glasses are huge pink tortoiseshell frames, and it looks like she hardly brushed her hair before she pulled it back in a ponytail. She isn't wearing any makeup and her ruddy face is like a

challenge. *I'm a mom; I'm too busy to bother with such silliness.*
Jane shifts in the recliner. Even the simplest movements look
complicated now, the way she has to push her palms against
the seat cushion to scoot herself forward or cup her hands
around the back of her thighs to lift her legs onto the footrest.
"I worry that I'll have some mama's boy if I let him into our
bed," she says.

"Don't be silly," Roz says from the loveseat. Roz is Jane's
newest friend and she's a lesbian and a know-it-all and she's
here with her pregnant girlfriend, which everyone is acting
nonchalant about. "They've had family beds in Asian countries
for centuries," she says.

Biz, the pregnant girlfriend, pats Roz's knee and nods. Jane
met these two in birthing class and talks about them all the
time now. Roz and Biz are going to try a water birth. Roz and
Biz are going to carry the baby around in a sling like people
do in Thailand. Roz looks like a lesbian, with the square jaw
and short, spiky hair. Biz is prettier, a slight girl with freckles
and watery blue eyes; her pregnancy looks like a joke, a beach
ball stuffed under a skinny girl's shirt.

Wendy starts to disagree with Roz, talking about parents
needing their alone time. The air is full of dust motes, and I
watch as they swirl wildly beneath the heat vents. Whenever
my parents used to have parties, I'd sit in the corner of the
couch, propped up by pillows, stupefied by the droning talk
about people I'd never heard of and places I'd never been.
I'd wait desperately, hopelessly for someone to break out
the board games or unlock a trunk of toys. Sandy makes a
comment from the couch about how it's to each his own. Roz
says to each her own, and Jane starts laughing.

I stare across the living room at Jane, but she's not looking
at me. She's nodding at Roz, waiting for her next comment.

Moira is still humming at my side; it sounds like "The Wreck of the Edmund Fitzgerald." I want Jane to look at me. I am leaning forward in my chair, willing her to look at me.

Jane and I met in ninth grade when all the middle schools poured into one high school; she sat kitty-corner from me in Algebra. I liked the way she surreptitiously carved up the top of her desk (*x = kill me now; Mr. Lehder is cockless*) and wore safety pins through her earring holes. She was the first girl I ever had a crush on. Not that I wanted to sleep with her; I just wanted to know her. And Moira came with Jane; they'd known each other since childhood, their houses four away from each other.

When Jane finally looks at me looking at her, her face is funny, as if she's got a question she's not asking, her brows knit, her head cocked to the side. I smile big at her. I'm trying to tell her something like *it's okay* or *good job* or *congratulations, baby.* She smiles back, but it looks bemused—tight-lipped, squinty-eyed, and I can see how it's the same smile she'll give her kid when he asks where babies come from or brings home some ugly macaroni and glitter glue art project.

"You know what?" she says loudly. "B.B. makes beautiful ceramics. That one's hers." She's pointing to my tall, curvy vase on the table against the far wall. She's been doing this all afternoon, making grand, awkward announcements about me and Moira, as if this were a blind date, Jane the matchmaker.

The vase is long, thin and ribbony, two smaller cylindrical arms curving upwards from the thick middle vessel. After my first trip to New Mexico, I came back and obsessively made a whole kiln of these, my saguaro series. The color came out wrong on this one, the individual glazes streaking red and blue when they were supposed to blend into an even lavender.

It was my wedding present to Jane and Darren. It looks out of place here now.

Jane once painted a mural over an entire wall of our dorm room, a psychedelic scene of students floating through the main artery of campus. The buildings were liquidy-looking, curvy walls and bulbous windows. The sky was deep violet, streaked with metallic silver stars. It was a shitty mural—the scale was off and the people looked cartoonish—but whenever we got stoned, we talked incessantly about becoming artists together, the loft we'd share in New York City. *SoHo*, we'd repeat, over and over again, the word slippery on our tongues.

My vase looks brash and adolescent now. Several pussy willow branches stick out from the top. Folk art, I once heard Jane call it. The only other art in here is a framed sketch of a sailboat design, the long beams and thick bolts exposed, scribbled measurements written along the perimeter. Darren loves sailboats. Darren is a high school guidance counselor, simple and sensitive enough to be considered boring. I hit on him a year ago, a drunken night when Jane was one long hallway away, and Ed and I were in the middle of almost splitting up.

"Is that what you do?" Roz says to me. "I mean, for a living?"

"Calls me on the phone all day," Moira says, laughing. "That's what she does."

"I'm a secretary," I say flatly.

"No you're not!" Jane yells. "B.B. had a First Thursday show at the Elizabeth Leach gallery last year."

"Two years ago," I say. "Two and a half."

"First Thursday," Jane repeats, more forcefully.

"I sold two pieces the whole time," I say, wishing she'd stop. "One was to my Uncle Sal. He keeps it in his bathroom, next to the decorative soaps." It comes out more sharply than I intended. Moira laughs, but everyone else is smiling quietly, except Jane, who looks at me with a lemon-faced sort of disapproval. There's another lull, but now it's laden with awkwardness. I feel like my ass is showing out the back of my skirt. I watch intently as a silver, pointy-nosed SUV drives past the picture window. I can sense the dappled red spreading up my neck.

"Secretaries are important," Biz finally says. Her voice is so girlish and silly, it's hard to imagine her as a lesbian or a mother. I don't know how to respond.

Moira keeps giggling softly next to me. "It's hot in here," she mutters and takes off her sweater, throwing it on the floor. Her wide nipples poke through her tank top, and her kneecaps are knobby and red below the hem of her miniskirt. The sweater lays crumpled at her feet like a lazy pet. "Aren't you hot?" she calls across the room to the co-workers in their elaborate sweaters. Her voice is starting to get slurry.

"No," Sandy of the Scottish terriers says quietly. Wendy doesn't answer. People stopped trying to make conversation with Moira a couple of Tom Collinses ago.

"Hot!" she repeats, fanning her red face with her fingers. "Jesus, Jane! You must be boiling under all that!"

Jane blinks at Moira, her lips pursed. Nadine leans over and sets a hand on Jane's shoulder, and Jane touches Nadine's fingers lightly. They nod wordlessly. There is something so casual and easy about the gesture, such a familiar intimacy, I have a hard time swallowing for a second. Nadine's always struck me as an unlikely friend for Jane because of her hemp clothing and earthy, wooden shoes. There's always a musk coming off her, from her hair or skin or breath. She was the sort of girl we made fun of in the dorms, the ugly, self-righteous kind who would narc on us for smoking out or playing our stereo too loud during quiet hours.

The last time I saw Jane was late in her second trimester. I took her to lunch at the Thai place on Burnside, where she asked the waiter an extraordinary number of questions, moving her finger along the menu from entrée to entrée, asking about cumin or chili peppers or peanut oil. The waiter's English was a stumbling, stammering attempt. A balding man in a corduroy suit jacket at the next table watched us. When the waiter finally left, Jane told me how pregnancy made her stomach so sensitive, she went for days wanting nothing but oatmeal and yogurt. I apologized for the restaurant choice, and she told me not to be silly, she loved it here. We talked until the food came. I told her about the trip Ed and I were planning to the coast, and the 23-year-old I'd read about whose porcelain sculptures were selling for $4000 apiece out of Pulliam Deffenbaugh (*the little fucker*, I was calling him), and the palette I'd dropped coming out of the kiln last week, destroying a whole swath of new work. "What was it?" she'd asked, and I tried explaining. "Tube people," I said, but the words felt immediately stupid and joke-like. I hated talking about my work because anything I said out loud made it seem ridiculous, like a silly little hobby, which in a depressing way, of course, it was. Jane told me about a woman she knew who was having so much trouble breastfeeding, her nipples were blistered and bleeding. Pus came out and she had to rub some sort of waxy lotion on them each night to try to heal them. It was a revolting story and the balding, corduroy man was watching us again.

When the food came, Jane picked out the green peppers and the cashews and baby corn, setting them along the edge of her plate. The way she chewed—loud and breathy—reminded me of a cow. She got some of the green curry on her cheek and I kept telling her where it was and she kept missing, so I leaned across the table to wipe it off. Jane's skin was so warm and soft. When she said, "Thanks, Bee," her breath was spicy on my face, and I jammed my toes in my shoes to quell the hot, thick feeling of sadness that was welling up. It reminded me of the time before we became friends, the months when I just watched her from across the classroom aisle, scared that the gulf between not knowing and knowing her would prove to be insurmountable, and I would be left alone to my bruised longing.

"Only one more month!" I say now, a little too loudly, raising my punch glass in the direction of Jane's belly.

Jane nods at me, her face softening a little. Everyone raises their glasses, adding onto the toast. There's laughter about something one of the lesbians said and I smile, as if I'd been listening.

"How 'bout you fix me another?" Moira says to me, swirling her glass, the ice clinking against the sides. Her armpits are unshaven. I can see white flecks of deodorant in the bushy patches of hair. The women of the circle stare at us. I pretend, improbably, not to hear her. Instead, I cough a fake cough, the noise low and unconvincing in my throat.

"I think it's game time," Nadine says as she pushes herself up from the rocker. "Bee-Bee," she says my name with a slow, ominous importance. "Would you like to come help me in the kitchen?"

The ice cubes still sit on the counter, sweating in their tray. I put them in the freezer, which is full of frozen dinners and Tupperware. One of the containers says *Tuesday* on it, another *Gazpacho*, the words lettered neatly on long strips of masking tape. Photos of Jane and Darren cover the front of the fridge:

the two of them on the top of South Sister; Jane flipping off the camera from bed, her face puffy and without make-up, her hair messed up; Darren in a red slicker, saluting from the stern of some boat. Darren's narrow face, deep-set eyes and ridged nose suggest a non-threatening masculinity, the kind you'd expect to see in an ad for insurance or anti-indigestion pills. In another picture, he's come up behind Jane and surprised her as she stands at their kitchen counter; the picture's blurry with motion, her head in midturn, her mouth partway open, both hands mittened in something pale and doughy on the counter. She has a streak of flour across one cheek.

I think of Jane since high school, first as a thrift store hipster, then later—in college—an arty stoner, then after graduation for a few years, an underemployed but devoted worker bee, and now, here, a wife, a mother-to-be. And always, with such success and ease to the reinventions, so little flourish, as if wherever she is in any single moment is where she always wanted to be. Each shift—even to here, to this boxy, bright neighborhood, and this boxy, bright kitchen—is unapologetic, unselfconscious, as if she is simply shrugging off a winter coat and putting on the lighter, better-fitting spring one.

Nadine calls me over to the table as she's pulling supplies from a used grocery bag like a magician from a hat—jars of baby food, paper plates, a bag of balloons. She hands me the balloons, then leans close and stage-whispers: "Is Moira okay?" The usual faint odor of sweat and dirt comes off her.

"She's fine," I say. "She's had a little too much to drink, but she'll be fine. She's had a rough time lately."

"Lately?" Nadine says, raising her eyebrow in an unexpectedly sly way.

Moira was convinced she was going to marry the guy who

got her pregnant six years ago, even though he was already married and a drunk. Since then, her affairs have become more cynical and ugly. For a while, she took to sleeping with different guys in her apartment building, bragging to me when she heard them talking about her in the hallway; she slept with one of the producers at the ABC affiliate after he interviewed her for a production-assistant job, and then sent him nasty, threatening letters when she didn't get hired. I stare at Nadine now, wondering how much Jane's told her about us.

"How's Ed?" she says, like she's reading my mind.

"Fine," I say. I picture Ed, slouched in his recliner, playing car-racing games on his PlayStation, his head weaving to the left and right with each curve. Ed makes decent money and cooks me ham and cheese omelets on Sundays and admires how many books I read. The shades will still be drawn when I stop by his apartment after this, and the room will smell unshowered. Saturdays, he says, are hygiene-optional days. When I lean over the back of the chair to kiss him, his hair will be thick with oil. Moira calls him a man-boy. He's got a beard, I tell her. He's balding, I say, even though I know that's not what she's talking about.

"You two talking about—?" Nadine waves her hand in the air. She's got a pursed, expectant look on her face—furrowed brows, a strange half-smile—the expression of righteous curiosity that domesticated women seem trained to fix on the unmarried, childless ones.

"A kitchen?" I say. "We don't talk much about kitchens." I am smiling, so as to appear nice and cleverly obtuse. "We should get back," I say because I don't want to have this conversation, not with Nadine. She doesn't strike me as someone who's been hazy about the difference between habituation and love, or at least not someone who'd ever admit to it.

"It's just a shame," she says, again with the stage whisper and nodding now toward the living room. We're back to Moira. "It's Jane's day." I stare at the crusty sleep in the corners of her eyelashes, magnified through her thick lenses, and I want to smack the smugness out of her; she is ancillary, I want to tell her, part of the detritus Jane has picked up along the way. There is no internal consistency to the group of women in the living room. They're not rooted in Jane's life like Moira and I are, even if Moira is all fucked up and drunk and I am me.

The night I hit on Darren, it was the last time we were celebrating something of Jane's—her promotion into mortgage-lending at the bank—several months before she got pregnant. Jane and Darren had moved out of downtown, and we'd come to a bar by their new place, one full of the neatly ordered tables, soft lighting and pale wood of suburbia. Photographs of Oregon landmarks lined each wall: Haystack Rock, Mt. Hood, Multnomah Falls. People around us ate complicated-looking appetizers and chicken-flecked salads.

We drank, telling boozy stories we'd told before—the time Jane got a ticket for flashing her boobs at a U2 concert, the time Moira shoplifted tire chains on a dare, the time I fell asleep during an Astronomy final. But the whiskey was giving me a headache and Moira kept trying to catch the attention of a goateed guy two tables away, and Jane's eyes were heavy; she kept leaning against Darren.

Our empty glasses stacked slowly into a messy centerpiece. I had the feeling we were going through the motions, replaying a version of this night we'd done before and more convincingly.

Darren and I ended up outside the bathrooms at the same
time, down a narrow hallway, just past the kitchen next to the
Emergency Exit door. We were having a hard time making
conversation. We always had a hard time making conversation.
I listened to the crackle of the deep fryers and the cooks
speaking in Spanish. Darren tapped his foot, staring past
me, his mouth partway open, as if he were about to speak.
"You watching the playoffs?" he finally said, and I didn't know
which sport he was talking about.

Behind him, rain slithered down the thick glass of the
Emergency Exit window. The walls were sponge-painted in
a pale blue pastel, the same lazy technique that seemed to
be everywhere recently, mottled streaks of paint across the
walls of restaurants, living rooms, clothing stores, as if people
could no longer be bothered with a brush. All at once, the
rain, the paint, the narrow hallway, they all filled me with the
slippery feeling that things were getting away from me, that
I was losing hold. And it wasn't just that I was drunk. It was
being in a strange restaurant in a strange neighborhood; it
was the seemingly endless tangle of fights that were waiting
for me back home (about Ed's obnoxious friends, my crappy
moods, his nosey mother, my dwindling sex drive); it was the
empty reminiscences that were likely passing for conversation
between Jane and Moira back at the table. I had the sudden
need to hold onto something, to bite down hard, to grasp
until my knuckles crackled.

Had one of the cooks come out from the kitchen, wiping
his hands on his food-stained smock, smelling of dish
detergent or heavy grease, maybe I would have grabbed onto
him. But no cooks came from the kitchen. And in two loping
steps, I was pressed up against Darren, saying, "Hi there,"
nuzzling his neck with the top of my head. When I raised

my face to his, though, his lips were tight against his teeth, like a dog readying to fight. Except he didn't look angry, he looked scared. I stumbled backwards, the booze clearing with a dizzying quickness. I kept saying, "Fuck," and "Shit," and, "Don't say anything." And then a smallish, white-haired man came out of the men's room, and Darren slipped quickly inside, mumbling at me, "Forget it," and "Okay," before closing the door on me, the smell of piss and minty air freshener fanning into the hallway.

Nadine makes all the guests stuff balloons up our shirts to give ourselves pregnant bellies. She's standing in the middle of the circle, yelling: "Think of it as an exercise in empathy!" Sandy and Wendy quickly fill their sweaters. Roz's balloon keeps slipping out of her loose T-shirt, revealing a thick patch of fuzz below her belly button. Moira takes two and makes them into tits instead. "I'm Pamela Anderson," she says. The balloons have the cheap, plastic taste of beach toys. Mine pulls at the skin of my stomach in a sticky, irritating way.

Next we get the paper plates. Nadine comes around with the baby food, scooping out different flavors. The game is to taste each and guess what food it is. Everyone acts disgusted, but in a playful way. The watery edges of each scoop bleed together in the center of the plate—oranges, greens, browns— like a poorly done abstract.

Moira is quiet beside me. When I look, her plate is resting on her knees and she is hunched over it, swaying slightly in her seat. Her red and blue balloon tits bulge out of the neck and arm holes of her tank top. A long strand of her hair is dangling dangerously close to the plate. I say her name— quietly—and she looks at me. Her chest heaves with her breath, and her eyes dart past me. When she finally fixes on my face, her expression is vacant. I've seen this many times before, the point in her drunkenness when she moves past histrionics and pulls inside herself to someplace darker.

"You don't have to play," I whisper, fighting my impatience. She stares at me like she doesn't hear, still hunched over.

I point to her plate. "You don't have to eat this."

She keeps looking at me, biting her bottom lip, suddenly seeming young. I think of the sleepovers we used to have in her attic, Jane and I sitting Indian style behind Moira, making cornrows. She'd turn around when we finished, and every time, I felt embarrassed by how different she seemed without her crazy, frizzy hair. Her eyes were suddenly buggy-looking, her cheeks dappled improbably pink. Not so tough, I used to think.

"Sit up," I say. She stares past me again. Jane is absorbed in the blank banter of the circle—someone's son's allergic to formula, someone else only bought organic baby food. Nadine yells, "Ready, set, go!" and everyone scoops the first spoonful into their mouths. Moira doesn't move. The orangey food tastes vaguely like perfume. People yell out carrots and peaches and sweet potatoes. It's sweet potato. There's small talk about sweet potatoes. Biz: "I always used to confuse the word yams and gams." Sandy: "A sweet potato has no relation to a potato, did you know that?"

We move onto yellow (banana guava blend) then purple (beets). The noise Moira's making now sounds less like humming and more like a low moan. "Jane," I say, cocking my head toward slumping Moira. Jane rolls her eyes, giving me a conspiratorial smile; it's not what I'm looking for. She goes back to yelling about spinach, her mouth wide open, murky and green. When she laughs, it's a brisk cackle, her big body shaking from the force of it: breasts, belly, everything.

Biz is shouting that it's sweeter than spinach. She thinks it's a fruit. Pear? Is it pear? Maybe it's pear? Biz's voice is shrill like a bird's.

Moira lets out a throaty growl. She sits up, smacking her lips together. Her cheeks are flushed, and a thin layer of grease brightens her forehead and her nose. One of the coworkers on the couch stares at her; so does Roz. When she says, "Fucking game," everybody looks. She suddenly stands and totters for a few moments, trying to get her bearings. It goes on for a few beats too long, like she's doing a strange, boneless dance for the crowd. "What're you looking at?" she calls out, loud and slurry, to the coworkers on the couch or Nadine; it's not clear who she's talking to.

Biz leans into Roz's side, looking like she might cry. Roz's face is taut, readied for a fight. Nadine shakes her head, saying Moira's name, which Moira ignores. The coworkers are wide-eyed, one with a hand to her face. Jane is simply staring, her expression unreadable, her eyes glossy and focused past Moira, who sways quietly in the middle of the room now, the red balloon escaping from the top of her shirt. "Gonlydan," she says and stumbles through the circle, leading with her head, tilting forward at the torso like a battering ram. Quick as that, she staggers out of the room and down the hallway. Gonna lie down, she'd been saying. We listen to the low creak of Jane and Darren's bedroom door, and then the groaning bedsprings.

For a minute, all is quiet, until Roz finally says, "Well!" in a quick sort of tone that means a lot more than well, and Wendy and Sandy and Nadine all laugh sharply, as if they're letting out a breath after holding it for too long.

Jane's got this beseeching, wide-eyed look to her. "Listen," she says, leaning farther forward in her chair, her belly drooping between her spread legs. For a moment, her lips move before words come out. She breathes deeply and slowly blinks as we all watch her, looking uncannily like someone waking from hibernation. It is a terrible and wonderful sight, Jane jarred momentarily loose of this strange life of hers, and I find myself clearing my throat and inching along my chair. It is—in one quick instant—the closest I've felt to her in years. And then, she says, "I'm really, really sorry, everyone," and she's shaking her head, sounding deflated. No, not deflated; she sounds ashamed.

After the gifts (the lesbians, a Thai sling; the coworkers, a stuffed panda and a soft-backed book about the primary colors; Nadine, a huge bag of hand-me-down clothes; me, a car seat, the third most expensive item on the registry; Moira, a onesie with the word Slugger written upside-down across the chest in purple fabric paint. She made it herself, the card explained, since it's unfair that words on baby clothes appear upside down from the baby's point of view), finally Sandy and Wendy stand from the couch and say they need to get going. Roz and Biz do the same. Everyone takes out their fake bellies.

"I need a ride," I say, suddenly realizing this. "Moira drove us. I don't know how to drive a stick. I mean, I guess we both need a ride."

There are discussions of neighborhoods and which direction we live, and the whole time I think Jane's going to jump in and volunteer, but in the end, it's Sandy and Wendy who agree.

In the bedroom, Moira's twisted onto her side, her face planted in the pillow, her legs splayed, the blue balloon still improbably lodged in her tank top, the red one lying next to her in the creases of the comforter. Jane and Darren's room is darker and woodier than the living room, the walls a deep green, the headboard a thick-grained cherry, the same as the dresser and end tables. The late afternoon light filters weakly through the blinds. Darren's green bottle of Polo cologne sits on top of the dresser by itself. He's been wearing the same cologne forever, and the smell embarrasses me. He never told Jane, and though he only kept the secret to save my ass, I still find a certain satisfaction in his withholding the information from her; it's the tiniest, most tender of betrayals. It makes me a sliver in the wood of their marriage. I'm embedded.

Moira makes a noise from the bed, a choking, watery snore. When I say her name, she doesn't move. I have to crawl on the bed and shake her a little. She wakes like a child, blinking quickly, looking around confused, rubbing her palms against her eyes.

"How long was I out?" she says.

"Not that long."

"Fuuuck," she says, the word a drawn-out sigh.

"You gotta get up. Those women from Jane's office are taking us home."

"I can drive."

"Shut up."

"Fuck you."

"Get up." I pull at her wrists. "You only have one boob left."

"Unicorn titty," she says. "Cyclops titty." She's sitting in the middle of the bed, unmoving. Her cheek is shiny from where she drooled. There's a half-dollar sized stain on the pillow.

"Come on," I say. "They're waiting. Wipe your face."

"You wipe your face," she says and then starts laughing.

"Come on, Moira."

"Little baby buggy bumper," she says.

"Get up."

"This little piggy went to market," she says.

"Jesus, Moira. Get up."

"Rock-a-bye," she says.

I pull at her wrists to get her up, and her whole body goes limp, her head lolling backwards. She laughs again, and it comes out a sloppy, gurgling noise. I watch the white skin of her neck, the tiny bumps of her spine. I want to press on the vertebrae. Not to hurt her, but to get a reaction. I squeeze both wrists hard and pull as forcefully as I can, which is satisfying, but Moira remains set in her place, implausibly resistant. I think of the black and white movies where the men slap the women, first across one cheek, then back across the other to snap them out of their hysteria.

"I'd be a good mom," Moira says, her head still tilted back.

"I know you would," I say, lying. When I let go of her wrists, my red fingerprints sprout from her skin.

"Maybe not as good as Jane, but good still," she says, and then lifts her head, looking at me beady-eyed, like she's waiting for me to challenge her.

For years, I was jealous of the childhood intimacy between Jane and Moira, the stupid words they'd made up together (*bam-bam* means penis, *pooter*, vagina, *fra-la*, to sleep in past your alarm—*I fra-la'd right through Calculus*), the casual way they had of drifting into each other's houses, the early birthday party pictures with one in the background while the other blew out candles. They were, for so long, each other's. I wonder now when Moira became mine.

"Fucking get up," I say and, finally, for some unknown reason, she listens.

In the backseat, she refuses to put on her seatbelt. "It chafes," she says. Sandy keeps watching us in the rear-view mirror.

"Thanks, Sandy," I keep repeating as Moira slumps over to my side of the seat, pressing her cheek against my arm, flopping her hands in my lap.

It's my least favorite time of day, when the light is dimming into evening, the sky gray, the streets shadowy, the streetlights tepid. It's the time of the day when I catch up to myself—sodden, regretful. I think of the way Jane and Nadine stood behind the screen door, watching us walk down the front porch, Sandy and Wendy several paces ahead, Moira clutching my elbow. Behind us, they waved and told us drive safe, Nadine standing there in just her stocking feet. I couldn't see her feet right then through the screen door, but I'd noticed moments before, as we'd said our goodbyes in the vestibule, all of us bundled in our coats, Nadine standing next to Jane without even her shoes on, shaking everyone's hands so officiously, like she'd just closed a business deal.

Sandy fiddles with the radio dial now, landing on a station playing a twangy song about love with a chorus about riding in a bus. Wendy is fixing her bangs in the mirror, picking at them with her thumb and pointer finger. "How's Daniel?" she asks Sandy. Sandy talks about Daniel starting softball this season.

"He sure looks big in his picture," Wendy says.

"I need to bring in a new one," Sandy says. "That's already two years old."

"Really? Two years."

The stilted quality to their conversation, it reminds me of a first date.

Moira rolls down her window; the air is cool outside and it whips through the backseat in a noisy whir. Sandy stares back at us. I lean across Moira and roll the window up a little while she whines, "No!"

"Shut up. Seriously," I whisper, and her mouth puckers like she's going to say something, but then her face goes slack, her eyes bleary and drunk.

"I like this song," Wendy says. Sandy agrees. The man on the radio has a deep, warbling voice. He reminds me of a yodeler. Wendy asks Sandy if she likes Shania Twain. Sandy says kind of and asks Wendy if she likes Alan Jackson. Next to me, Moira's finally quiet, her eyes closed, her mouth hanging open just slightly, the back of her head resting against the seat.

"I like that one remake," Wendy says about a song I've never heard. "I'm not sure I know that one," says Sandy. They have the tentativeness of new friendship, the halting tenderness of people who haven't yet been terrible to each other.

The cold air riffles the top of Moira's hair. I listen to the breath out of her mouth, a slow, whispery stream that catches when we go over big bumps. I think of all the days we spent high and stupid in Jane's shitty apartment, curled up on her ragged couch, laughing at nothing, listening to the Cocteau Twins and Morrissey. I think of the afternoons we slathered on baby oil and stepped through her bedroom window onto the sloping roof, lying on the tarred shingles in our bikinis, Jane's hips vast and curvy, Moira's bony as hell, me right in the middle.

Moira's hand lies damp and limp on the seat between us; when I lace my fingers through hers, I can feel her heart beating in her palm. It's miles till we're home, and her pulse slows as we sit at stoplights and wind through familiar streets. Sandy keeps watching us in the mirror, Moira sleeping, me hanging on.

survival tips: toddler birthday party

DON'T THINK ABOUT fire tornadoes. Don't think about the insurrectionist who wore horns and turned out to be vegan. Don't think about the domestic supply of infants. Go to the Dollar Store and buy bubble wands, gummy bracelets, *Doc McStuffins* Grab N Go Play Pack Coloring and Sticker Set, *Frozen 2* Grab N Go Play Pack Coloring and Sticker Set, *Encanto* Grab N Go Play Pack Coloring and Sticker Set.

Invite everyone from the preschool. Invite neighbor kids. Invite kids from the park who aren't technically friends with your toddler but aren't not friends. They go down the slide together. They swing. They spin each other on the large, cockeyed, plastic ring that is the replacement for the too dangerous metal merry-go-round. Not everyone will come and better to have a too-full house than you, your toddler, your husband and all those fucking cupcakes.

Make adult drinks. Offer all the Moms—and the one Dad (man bun and egregious levels of lauding)—"daytime sangria" and don't be insulted when more than a few decline. These are not your friends. You make friends through sarcasm and shared history. These are sleep-deprived strangers.

Set up Pin the Tail on the Donkey. Set up Water Balloon Toss. Set up Piñata. Say, "Who wants to do?" "Who wants to do?" "Who wants to do?" Wave your arm like the balloon man in front of the auto dealership. The shine of all those windshields in the summertime always makes you wish you'd remembered your sunglasses.

Drink your daytime sangria. Laugh with everyone when blindfolded three-year-olds wield baseball bats dangerously yet ineffectively at Donkey from *Shrek*, a movie your child has not seen yet only because they do not sit long enough to watch movies. Be grateful that the toddler who refuses the blindfold is not your toddler. Be grateful that the toddler who cries when the one Dad with the man bun smashes Donkey with a single, powerful swing is not your toddler.

Argue quietly in the kitchen with your husband (two Dads at the party) about the cupcakes. He wants to serve them outside. You, inside. You do not care but you argue because you are tired and slightly buzzed and would like to get bent over the arm of your living room sofa by the one Dad with the man bun.

Catch sight of your toddler and your deaf, geriatric Manx in a midday sunbeam, one chubby hand on the cat's rump. Marvel at the patience of your cat. Marvel at the beauty of your toddler. Tell your husband to get the camera. Know your mistake is in not telling him look. Feel bad that he was busy finding his camera and missed it.

Serve the cupcakes inside. Lie when a mother who is not your friend asks if you made them. Shout "In all my spare time!" without meaning to shout and feel bad for the face the mother who is not your friend makes.

Try to keep the toddlers at the table while they eat. Try to get the parents to wipe toddler hands and faces. Watch the toddlers get frosting on the sofa you'd like to be bent over. Say to your husband, "You were right," and know this is the currency of marriage. Know you don't really want to be bent over the sofa. Know you want to want it. Know you only want to sit on the toilet without anyone trying to open the bathroom door.

Think you will remember all of this. Forget that memory is happenstance and sometimes cruel. Forget that scientists have proven memory is impressionistic, whole swaths lost. Do not know this is a whole swath: the daytime sangrias, Donkey, the sunbeam, the indoor cupcakes. Do not realize this will become only pictures in a hardbound photobook from the hardbound photobook website where you also order your year-end photo card, the three of you, posing arm in arm year after year, smiling, trying not to blink at the same time, trying not to blink at all, blinking.

big home

HOGAN MET LILY over the phone. He'd always had a thing for girls with flower names. In high school, he'd mooned silently over a bookish Rose for months and months—close to a year—with her brightly patterned blouses, expertly parted hair, a scar beside her lip that resembled a tiny sickle, as if trying to cleave her mouth in two. He loved the protective way she snaked her arm around her exams, the slow sashay she took to the teacher's desk upon finishing (often first), presenting the paper in two outstretched arms, a gift.

Later, during his single semester of college, he happened upon Jasmine who worked behind the reference desk in the library and always smelled faintly yet alluringly of sweat and menthol. He liked the way she chewed on the end of her pen. He had seen her, more than once, stick the wrong end in her mouth, then spit it out quickly, looking around to see if anyone had caught her. Often, he would come up with arcane topics (mourning rituals of pachyderms; trade routes in sixteenth century Timbuktu) so he could steal five, ten minutes of her time; once, she even came out from behind her desk and walked the third-floor stacks with him, searching for a missing issue of the *Journal of Military History* and its article on unclaimed West Virginian Civil War medals.

Jasmine wore sandals, and they made a sibilant sound against the floor as she walked beside him. Hogan fought the urge to hold her hand, a decision that he had, to this day, regretted. On warm, friendless Sundays, or when he was caught behind an exhaust-heavy truck on the 880 into San Jose for work, or in bed at night, as his radiator ticked tunelessly, Hogan reimagined the last dozen years of his life, from the moment he successfully laced Jasmine's fingers through his: wrought-iron patio furniture, punch bowls filled with bright concoctions of floating fruit, a couch with cushions long molded to the matching imprints of their asses.

He met Lily on a Tuesday, statistically the slowest day at the Call Center. Hogan was packing—old file folders, paperweights—for an office move in August. "All *you* have to do," Marcus had announced this morning, delivering a stack of boxes to Hogan's cubicle, "is pack. *We* take care of the rest." Marcus was a company man—Hogan considered himself a company man, too, his tenure triple Marcus's—though Marcus was militantly upbeat in a way that made Hogan gnash something. His teeth? It felt deeper than his teeth. This was Hogan's second move with TRS. The first offices had been airy and light filled. There'd been snack machines in the lobby and a break room. Now the coffee pot sat on the desk in one of the empty cubicles. You had to go to the bathroom sink to fill the carafe.

"What do I pack," Hogan asked, "six weeks in advance?" He wasn't being difficult. It was a genuine question.

Marcus suggested inessentials. He had a strong jaw, the face of a man easily loved.

Hogan was taking down postcards from his best friend, Leon, when his TTY machine trilled. Leon had worked for years in the next cubicle, back before smart phones and WhatsApp and SMS. He'd moved to England with his wife shortly after being laid off, a turn of events that was never not surprising to Hogan. Up and moving to England was the kind of thing people did in a Netflix series. It was the kind of thing college kids did or young single ladies. Leon's postcards were uniformly cheesy (double-decker buses, Buckingham Palace guards in beehive hats) which Hogan had at first thought was meant to be ironic since Leon wasn't a tourist, though they'd kept coming: Big Ben. Trafalgar Square. Windsor Castle.

Hogan answered the call, typing "CA TRS 9109M. Number Calling Please?" into the TTY machine. CA for California; TRS for Telephone Relay Service; 9019, his identification number; M for male. Some mornings, he woke to find himself silently reciting the line, as if he'd mistaken his alarm for the phone.

A quick row of ten numbers appeared on the TTY's LCD screen. Hogan recognized the area code as Monterey, and when he called, a man answered in a gravelly voice, as if he'd just woken at nearly two in the afternoon. Hogan announced: "California Relay Services. I have a call from a hearing-impaired party."

"From Lily?" the man said, clearing his throat then coughing.

"From Lily?" Hogan typed into the TTY machine. He was struck, immediately, by the loveliness of the name, though of course he didn't comment; it was forbidden for Relay Operators to participate.

"Who else?" the TTY caller typed back. "Miss my ass, or what?"

Hogan recited the words, verbatim.

The man laughed, then said, "Sure as hell do. What do you think?" and Hogan typed.

"I think you wish I was next to you right now, naked in your bed," Lily typed.

Hogan could feel a light flush of embarrassment as he spoke the words, though he was a professional; he'd been a relay operator for eleven years and understood how quickly he, as a person with independent thoughts and feelings, became invisible to the callers. He was not Hogan. He was 9109 M, one more piece of hardware, not unlike a closed caption decoder or a smoke alarm that flashed a bright strobe when tripped.

Most callers, however, didn't talk like this. Conversations were brief, stripped of pleasantries and chitchat, especially on the day shift. Day shift meant business hours. To Aegis Assisted Living: like to set up a tour. To Oak Ridge elementary: second grader out with strep. To Dr. Wilbanks: persistent nerve pain in the left elbow.

But Lily and the man, whose name turned out to be, plainly, Thomas, talked for a full twenty-seven minutes, meandering through a broad range of topics, from the tequila Thomas had drunk too much of the night before, to Lily wondering if she should get a nose job (to which Thomas yelled, and Hogan typed capital N, capital O), to the last time Thomas came to see her and left a wet spot the size of a bowling ball in the middle of her bed. "I believe *you're* the one who left that," Thomas said.

"I'm bored," Lily typed at one point. "My nipples are hard."

Hogan found her disarming and refreshing and he pictured her as a redhead, maybe with a slight curl to her hair which she ran one finger absently through. He thought she was dimpled, but not round-faced. He imagined a sleekness to her features, the confident maturity of having been around the block a time or two, but not in a slutty way. A liberated way.

"Bye, babe," she typed simply, without warning or apology soon after Thomas finished a long story about his dog throwing up on his carpet.

"Love you, Doll," Thomas said, and Hogan found a quick, throaty thrill in the typing.

On that first night, he thought of Lily only briefly as he sat at his kitchen counter, eating soup. His refrigerator hummed a loud, angry hum, and Hogan wondered if Lily was eating dinner now too, and if so, alone or with someone else? Was she dressed in work clothes or stripped down to a robe, her bare legs exposed, one crossed over the other and swinging through the air? These were lazy, reflexive sort of thoughts, a fleeting indulgence; he barely even realized he was thinking them.

When there was a knock on his apartment door, it was Mr. Orachuk from across the hall. His pilot light was out, and he needed Hogan to bend down and light it. Mr. Orachuk was old and curled in on himself, a question mark of a man who used walls and doorways to steady his legs instead of the walker that sat in the far corner of his apartment, pushed between a waterless aquarium and a tall stack of magazines.

Hogan knelt on the kitchen linoleum and leaned into the mouth of the stove. Mr. Orachuk stood by, complaining congenially of his hip problems and his terrible son back in detox after another run of cocaine and barbiturates. His hearing aid was buzzing a one-note alarm and the oven gave off the deep odor of years of burnt dinners. More than once, Hogan had run across the hall to disarm the smoke alarm and rescue a smoldering casserole from its depths.

After Hogan lit the pilot, Mr. Orachuk offered him a glass of tap water. Hogan wasn't thirsty, but he accepted. Mr. Orachuk was on a roll now, reminiscing about the lantern fish he used to have. Did Hogan know lantern fish? Yes, Hogan knew lantern fish from their previous conversations about lantern fish.

"What happened to the Black fellow?" Mr. Orachuk said. Mr. Orachuk always wanted to know what happened to Leon, who had once come over with Hogan to pull the alarm down from the ceiling while Hogan carried charred remains of fish sticks down the stairs and into the parking lot dumpster.

"England," Hogan said, as he always said, and it was in moments like these when he most missed Leon: the way Leon would sprawl loose-limbed on Hogan's couch after work with a beer, as happy to flip through the cable channels as to talk. Hogan missed Leon's way of keeping conversations afloat while making surprisingly little demands on the other person. Leon could deliver deft monologues on how terribly the Kings were doing this season, what the real solution was to the problems in the Middle East (parachuting a whole army of laptops into rural villages), if he was ever going to want kids with the same urgency that his wife did. Time became languid when Leon was around, not something Hogan had to fight against, willing the seconds to move faster as he stood downwind of an old man's creaky breath.

"Your hearing aid," Hogan said, pointing to his own ear.

"What?"

"You need a new battery," he shouted, handing Mr. Orachuk back the water, unsipped.

"What?"

"Your hearing aid."

"What?"

Lily called again on Thursday, mid-morning, to a fellow in Berkeley. Not Thomas. Dwayne. They bantered about mutual friends (pregnant Barb, Lou who just lost his job). They told private jokes (one to do with a pet iguana, another with the inexplicable punch line of New Haven). Dwayne and Lily griped about their jobs (Dwayne, a bartender who had to make needlessly complicated drinks for yuppies in the East Bay. Lily, a hospital nursing aid).

I swear, she typed, *O'Donnell is taking years off my life.* Hogan recognized O'Donnell as a San Jose hospital, all the way on the other side of town as the Call Center, but still, might he and Lily swerve to avoid the same potholes on the same city roads? Might they look out their windows at the end of their shifts at the same pallid sunsets? *Swing shift is fucking me up. Can't figure out my days.*

Hogan liked that. If asked, he too couldn't figure out his days, especially the part after work and before bed, or the part between calls, or the part after breakfast and before work and nothing good on TV and too early to stream Netflix without getting depressed.

Lily told a story about accidentally getting mail at her house for some guy on the next block and reading a letter from his ex-wife where she called him a shitbag cocksucker. Dwayne told her she was going to hell for snooping. "Among other offenses," Lily typed. There was something effortless in her glowing green words, and unexpected too, Hogan with no idea what might come next; he liked that.

"I miss you," Lily typed. "When am I going to see you? I want to touch you."

Dwayne told her, "I'm not sure, babe." He had his sister and two nephews coming to stay for a week.

Lily typed "..." in response.

"She's speechless," Hogan said. Those brief moments when he had to interpret what had been typed, rather than recite it, were awkward for him. The shift was a subtle one, the way Lily became a *she*, Hogan the mediator. They were the times when he felt most like the eavesdropper.

"Soon," Dwayne said, without pause. "Tell her, soon." The man spoke with such conviction, Hogan felt a flood of emotions: again, the sheepishness of the interloper, but also jealousy.

Marcus brought in cupcakes for Peggy's birthday month. Fred and Peggy, the last remaining day-shifters, stood at their desks, the cubicle walls only chest high. Everyone held up the cupcakes, as if toasting. Hogan didn't really know Peggy. She was the third most senior relay operator, moved from overnight to day in the last round of shuffling and layoffs. For years, Hogan's primary impressions of Peggy—and all the other swing and overnighters—had come from the personal items peopling their cubicles. Peggy collected Beanie Babies, giving Hogan the idea that Peggy would be childish and silly. She was instead quiet and efficient. He wondered if his postcards had given her the impression of a worldly sophisticate.

Next came Guy the following week, Hogan regretting what he'd chosen to put in boxes, spending a remarkable amount of time looking for his good pen, his stack of Post-Its. He didn't consider himself a person with lots of cubicle detritus until asked to gather it. Eleven years of file folders. Of alligator clips. Of gel pens. Of rubber bands. Of cheap grocery store tea. In the new space, they would be sharing cubicles. They could bring essential personal items. Hogan didn't know what an essential personal item was. A shared cubicle felt generally and uncomfortably communistic; would his cheap grocery store tea become property of everyone? Would he get a designated drawer in the file cabinet, a discrete section of the cubicle wall? Marcus was giving up an office and an office door. "An open floor plan," he repeated. And: "Above a Subway." Hogan was stuck now with a clotting ballpoint.

Guy worked in an animal shelter in Santa Cruz and told earnest stories about three-legged dogs. Lily was finally getting acclimated to leaving for work at 3pm and not being home till after midnight. *My cicadian rhythm is retraining itself.* Hogan spoke without correcting to *circadian*; not his place, and he liked that Lily got it wrong, liked the idea of her 17-year hibernation, only to emerge as an all-consuming force.

Relaying her calls reminded Hogan of the call center heyday, when he was the last best stopgap between a person and complete isolation. The fact that technology had raced so quickly and comprehensively past him had felt personal, making Hogan generally distrustful of tech. His mother had cajoled him onto Facebook, though he never posted. She was a manic poster of inspirational quotes (*dance like no one is…*) and out-of-focus bingo night photos from her retirement community and #tbt of Hogan as a brace-faced teen, clasped to her side.

Lily told Guy about her recent house-sitting stint, when she managed to simultaneously clog her friend's toilet (*If you could've seen the size of that colossal shit*, she typed, Hogan marveling at her fearlessness) and let the chihuahua, Giovanna, escape out the back door. Lily ran around the neighborhood frantic, shining her flashlight under every hedge and behind every garbage can, squawking for the dog (that's how she referred to herself, *squawking*), arriving back home sweaty and weepy and exhausted from sprinting for blocks, full of the panic and dread of having deeply fucked up, only to find Giovanna wading along the bathroom floor, up to her belly in the dirty water that had been overflowing for nearly an hour.

She had a cockeyed smile, Hogan decided, the sort that confused people about whether she was serious or sarcastic. She enjoyed that confusion and wasn't quick to put people at ease. She liked to watch people squirm for a bit. Lily, he guessed, was a step ahead of most people. She made it so easy—the banter, the sly, self-deprecating confidence. She only talked in stories. Hogan wasn't sure if he was growing more enamored of her or of being her.

Marcus hoisted old file cabinets onto hand trucks, disgorging them from unused cubicles and lining them along the east wall. It was a loud process, full of grunting. Beside the cabinets, Marcus wheeled over the wobbliest and screechiest of the desk chairs. In the seats of several desk chairs, he piled tangles of outdated headsets. He was culling. He ran a ring of blue painter's tape around the objects. *No move*, he'd written on printer paper with sharpie. *No move. No Move. No Move,* he taped around the clump.

He heard Peggy one day: "I can do that red skirt you love. You remember that park we used to go to? The one with the angry geese?"

It had to be Lily. Who else with the red skirt? Who else with the angry geese? Hogan had never "fallen in love." He was 38 years old and increasingly skeptical of the concept. His relationships had been few and far between: Joy-Marie who'd let her little poodle eat out of her hand and started most stories with, "I have a funny story." Sylvia, who'd moved into the apartment beneath his after her divorce and taken his virginity like a librarian taking an overdue book, with quick, determined efficiency and a startling lack of flourish. Denise, who was obsessed with yoga and had a living room furnished with beanbag chairs and mattress-like couches that lolled on the floor, giving the whole relationship a lazy, shapeless feel.

But now ("Let's go and throw stale bread at dumb waterfowl") he thought maybe falling in love was simply pattern recognition: you anticipate a person, the person delivers upon that anticipation, you are rewarded with a surge of knowing. A surge of knowing felt something like home. Not *home* home. Hogan was no huge fan of his apartment. The other kind of home. Big home. It was wild to have a woman relaying Lily, like Lily was in the room with him.

"I have," Lily said, "a whole sleeve of English muffins. English muffins are easily the worst bread. Why even?"

There were five men in all. Aside from Thomas and Dwayne and Guy, Hogan knew about Fumio in the East Bay, a poet with a Japanese accent, making relaying embarrassing as Hogan dumbly asked him to repeat words (*Rerise, RE-rise, RERISE,* Fumio would shout). Carl from Salinas was often on the cell phone in his car, the conversation sprinkled with invective toward other drivers, which Hogan was duty-bound to relay, making for several exchanges when Lily mistakenly thought Carl was calling her a douchebag or a cunthole.

Hogan learned details of Lily's life: her dad was dead. She was "half-Buddhist, half-Jewish, half-Atheist." She lived in a studio apartment over an old couple's garage in Ben Lomand. She had thirty percent hearing in one ear if she wore a clunky yellow hearing aid, which she did only at work. She worked four days on, three days off, and when she complained of San Jose's choking traffic and dingy, faceless buildings (*That town was built by some sick sadist*), Hogan felt he might just burst from affinity and understanding.

Then came a clot of days when the calls stopped. It wasn't unusual for there to be a three, four-day gap. But now it was a week, eight days. Nine. Hogan swallowed down feeling. Marcus told them to put green dot stickers on everything needing moving from their cubicle. Hogan green dotted his chair, his computer, the TTY machine. Marcus kept coming by to check on the progress of the green dotting. Hogan wanted his garbage can, didn't he? Hogan wanted his bulletin board, didn't he?

The *No Move* pile grew and grew so that the painter's tape came to represent only the nucleus. Newest additions: several whiteboards; rolled-up clear carpet protectors; stacks and stacks of desktop file organizers; the huge wall components of three entirely disassembled cubicles. Hogan had never considered that the cubicles could—or should—be dissembled. He'd thought the cubicles had come with the place. Long unused desks now sat exposed, surrounded only by permanent grooves in the carpeting.

A few times, Peggy sidled over to the *No Move* pile. Once, she made her way close enough to open a file cabinet drawer and then another, peering inside. Later, in the coffee cubicle (the coffee maker green dotted, the powdered creamer container green dotted, the tray of mugs green dotted–the tray and the mugs both), Hogan said to Peggy, "Kind of sad."

Peggy looked at him blankly.

Hogan nodded to the *No Move* pile. "Like the island of misfit toys," he said.

"What?" Peggy said.

"I saw you," he said. "Looking." They had spoken to each

other before. They'd said hellos, goodbyes. He'd wished her a happy birthday. It wasn't like this was their first conversation. "I saw you looking inside the file cabinets."

"People leave stuff." She shrugged. "Magnets," she said. "Keys."

1:49 on a Wednesday and Hogan had never been so happy to relay *wake up motherfucker* to Dwayne. Oh Dwayne! It was so Dwayne to sleep half the day away after tending bar! Hogan wanted to laugh but he didn't laugh. Of course he didn't laugh. He was convinced his force of want had made this call happen on his shift, in his queue, even if his force of want had not made this call happen on his shift, in his queue for the preceding ten days, his force of want impervious to logic.

Thursday morning, and it was Guy who'd left his iPad on Lily's nightstand. *I drew penises on all the photos of your wife*, she typed. Thursday afternoon–two in one day!–and Carl wanted to know what she was wearing. So many cubicle walls had come down around Hogan and Peggy and Fred, Hogan's voice echoed more than usual.

"Your t-shirt," he told Carl. Carl wanted to know what else. Hogan knew Lily would type *nothing else*. Lily typed *nothing else*.

Friday—moving day—and men in waist belts carted out desks and chairs and cabinets and drawers. There was a choreography to how phone lines would be ported without an interruption in services, which involved the three of them continuing to take calls as the office moved out from under them. Fumio was saying about writer's block and the trouble with allergies.

I didn't know you had allergies, you poor thing, Lily typed. *To what?*

"Ay-a-gees!" Fumio said.

"Allergies?" Hogan asked. The movers grunted at each other. They hoisted and smelled rank. Sweat and exertion.

"Ay-a-gees!"

"I'm sorry," Hogan said, unaccustomed to being bad at his job. The movers left *No Move* untouched. Poor *No Move*, Hogan thought.

Fumio had to spell the word.

Correction from 9019M: Hogan typed. *Elegies*.

No worries, Lily typed. *9019M*, she typed.

That night, as he sat in his apartment, he heard a loud, shattering crash of glass. He ignored it, as he'd trained himself to do with all manner of noise from the tenant parking lot beneath his windows. For a full beat or two, he continued to watch a documentary about an orphaned polar bear cub being raised by humans, until he realized the sound had not come from outside but from in the building. Hogan moved faster than he had in weeks, maybe months.

He ran across the hall, first knocking on Mr. Orachuk's door, then banging hard, then calling the old man's name, then returning to his own apartment for Mr. Orachuk's spare key. Inside the old man's apartment, there was the same stale, unwashed smell as usual, but with something layered on top of it now, tangy and metallic, which Hogan couldn't identify until he stepped into the living room. In the far corner lay Mr. Orachuk, crumpled among huge shards of glass and a littering of the tiny pebbles that had lined the bottom of the waterless aquarium. One of the old man's legs was twisted into an incomprehensible angle; blood (that was the smell) oozed quickly from cuts along his face and arms. On its usual shelf, what remained of the aquarium–three sides still intact and impotent (more impotent than usual)—and the front one gone, nothing left but a few jagged teeth along the bottom, stubbornly hanging on.

"Mr. Orachuk," Hogan yelled, wishing he could remember the man's first name. Had he ever known his first name? He stepped through the glass and grabbed Mr. Orachuk's arm, feeling for his pulse, as he had seen so many people in so many movies do, and called 911.

When the ambulance arrived, Hogan instinctively lied to a paramedic and said yes, he was family, so that he could go along. He was not ready to separate from the old man, could not fathom a quiet return to his own apartment. During the ride, he kept touching Mr. Orachuk's shoulder, a nervous gesture he couldn't stop repeating. "Looks like a stroke," one of the paramedics told him. "Sure did himself in on that fall, though. Terrible luck."

As the paramedics jammed tubing deep into Mr. Orachuk's throat and swabbed his cuts, Hogan wondered had it been luck? Had Mr. Orachuk been simply, unfortunately walking past the aquarium when the stroke hit, or had he been standing over it, maybe peering in, contemplating the lantern fish that once inhabited it, the leafy green plants swaying in the filtered tide, the fake copper scuba divers, all gone now, lost to him, like so much of Mr. Orachuk's shitty, sad, old life?

The driver called out "nine-minute ETA to O'Donnell Med Cen." Or maybe it was the paramedic in the back; Hogan would wonder about that later. Who had first spoken the words? When exactly had he realized, as they whirred through the dark streets, that they were heading to Lily's hospital?

In the days that followed, Hogan would remind himself more than once that his initial impulse had been charitable, that those first minutes of panic and chaos were selfless, his motives unmuddied. Because once he heard *O'Donnell*, everything went askew. Maybe it was the adrenaline already pulsing through him or the wailing of sirens overhead or the stomach-churning dips and swerves of the road, but almost instantly, in the span of that one word, Hogan forgot Mr. Orachuk—strapped to a backboard as he was, spotty with orange ointment, mouth agape from plastic tubing—and grew certain, instead, that it would be his own body to fly apart, his own organs to fail, from the force of hurtling headlong—surely, he was sure of it—into his fate.

He sat trapped in a ridiculous outfit, a coat hastily thrown over a t-shirt and shorts, and worst of all, white socks in sandals, as he sat in an unforgiving waiting room chair. He was cold and embarrassed, and felt a particular scorn for his knobby, hairy kneecaps, especially as a tiny blonde passed through the waiting room, wearing the same orange scrubs he'd heard Lily describe more than once (*You think it's a coincidence they make us dress like inmates?*); or, later a brunette with spotty, flushed cheeks and an ample behind; or, still later, a pale-faced, skinny girl working her hair into a rubber-band, and he asked himself the same hiccupping question:

Her?

Her?

Her?

After several hours, he was ushered to the ICU waiting room where the chairs were replaced with vinyl couches. The adrenaline had steadily seeped out of him, replaced by a deep, achy restlessness. What had he thought, that she would come running as he stepped through the hospital doors, her hands flying around her face in a flurry of sign language that he would suddenly, intuitively understand?

Finally, when the clock on the far wall read 3:12, a doctor told Hogan that Mr. Orachuk (Charles, of course, that was his first name, Charles) was unconscious but stabilized and in serious condition; all signs indeed indicated a stroke, but the fall had done its own host of damages: a crushed windpipe, deeply lacerated arms and chest, loss of blood. "It's good you found him when you did," the pale-faced doctor said. Then: "You can see him now."

Hogan was surprised by the offer. See him? He felt compelled to fess up, ever the interloper, but was too ashamed to do anything but walk to the room number he'd been given. Machines growled and gave off strange light at the head of Mr. Orachuk's bed. Mr. Orachuk lay swaddled in a mummy-like coating of bandages, which seemed to glow in the dark of the room. The bright stench of ammonia hung in the air, but nearer to Mr. Orachuk's bed was the faintest remnant of the old man's apartment, that familiar, slightly sweet odor of rot.

Hogan found the Subway. He could see the second floor from the sidewalk but not how to get there.

"How do you get upstairs?" he asked the girl in the Subway.

"Upstairs?" the girl said. There were no customers. It was 7:54 a.m. The smell of cheesy bread—or something tangy and unspecified—was not good. He could feel it lodging in his nose hairs and feared it lingering, just as the dread taste of the hospital had clung to the back of his throat in bed. He'd barely slept.

He ended up calling into the service, Fred answering, "California telephone relay services, number calling, please." It felt queer and upside down, being the caller. Fred laughed when Hogan asked how to get in. "The office is a shithole," he said, gleefully. Hogan had to go half a block down, past the State Farm office.

Hogan kept dropping sentences, barely listening as he relayed that Janice needed her Diazepam from the pharmacist. That Hilde needed to change her ticket to Bethesda. The new office was a shithole, small and cramped, Peggy's voice bouncing off Fred's bouncing off Hogan's. The low nap carpet was spongy. Marcus ran around with the box cutter, rooting out the gooseneck lamps, the extra staplers, notepads. Packing peanuts clung to his sleeve.

Lily didn't call, Hogan paranoid that he'd caused her silence by having trespassed into her territory. A sleepless dread moved through him. The only windows were south-facing and poorly insulated. The sun cooked them. Marcus got them Subway for lunch. Hogan regretted his pickles.

When work finally ended and he drove home through poorly timed left turn lanes that were not yet his, he was only home long enough for a new shirt, new layer of deodorant, and a power bar. Back at the hospital, he found himself unsure of what to do. He sat in the chair next to Mr. Orachuk's bed and thrummed his fingers on his thigh. Mr. Orachuk looked small in his bed, his legs twigs beneath the blanket. The bandage taped across his throat reminded Hogan almost quaintly of a neckerchief. Each time anyone entered the room—nurse, orderly, doctor, janitor—Hogan startled slightly in his seat, tasting his pulse in his throat. But they turned out to be men, or far too old, or far too young, or quick to turn their head when he said, "Hi," very softly from his seat, which he had taken to doing with the women in orange scrubs.

It was a terrible plan, he realized, sitting here like this, waiting, no different than sitting in the new office waiting for her call. What were his options? Go up to a charge nurse

and ask for Lily? Walk the hallways, floor by floor, looking
for the girl with the clunky yellow hearing aid? And then
what? What was he supposed to say? "You don't know me,
but I know you?" "Now I know this might sound crazy...?"

Mr. Orachuk made a low groan, and Hogan peered at the
bed. But it was nothing; the old man lay still, unmoving.
Hogan placed a hand lightly on his forehead, and then on
the crown of his head, petting the hair that would soon turn
greasy but, for now, was still soft as a child's.

The first Lily call in the new office was Thomas. He wanted
to go see *Spiderman*, Lily wanted the horror movie with the
girl and the cult and the flowers. She couldn't remember
the name. He didn't want a horror movie. He hated horror
movies. What about *Shazam*? Fuck, why did it have to be a
superhero movie, Lily wanted to know.

The call hit Hogan wrong. It wasn't a good call; could have
been any two people bickering about movies. He expected
something different of Lily, but maybe it was him, coiled
tight from his nightly vigil and wanting to scream out so
badly into the phone. Hogan's shared cubicle turned out to be
blunt and impersonal, except for Rick from nightshift's one
wedding photo from a bygone era, his wife's sleeves puffed
at the shoulders, her veil a headband.

Sometimes at O'Donnell, he walked boldly to the vending
machines or the bathrooms or even once to the cafeteria,
swinging his arms at his sides, watchful as a periscope.

But mostly, he sat beside Mr. Orachuk, reading aloud from
the pulpy sections of newspaper he'd found littered through
the waiting room, or watching the slow, steady red trail of
a heartbeat as it slunk across the monitor, googling Mr.

Orachuk's junkie son, though there were too many and not enough Orachuks.

One night, back from the hospital, his phone startled him as he was falling asleep in front of Animal Planet. As accustomed as he was to this sound at work, he was just as surprised by it here.

"Buddy!" It was Leon. They rarely spoke. Leon called every several months, but between the time difference and the rounds of phone tags, it wasn't unusual for the attempts to peter out to nothing. Hogan couldn't even remember the last time.

"Fine," Hogan said. It'd been swamp wranglers when he'd nodded off. Now it was emergency room vets. "Good," though what he wanted to say (which he didn't realize he wanted to say till he heard Leon's good-natured, familiar congeniality) was I'm worn down, soggy, tired. "How are you?"

"I wake you?" Leon said, and Hogan lied. Leon talked about their flat (that's what he called their apartment), his wife's PhD program (something to do with economics that Hogan ever only tenuously understood), the soccer team he was following, Totten something, which Hogan had never heard of. He'd only ever watched sports because Leon liked to.

"How's the rain?" This was what he always asked.

Leon was breaking up. "You're breaking up," Hogan told him. Leon was saying something. "–hear me?"

Hogan could hear him. "The call center moved," he said. Hogan told him about the new place and about only Fred and Peggy still there.

"What else you been up to?" Leon said.

Hogan was not overly fond of this question. "My neighbor had a stroke."

"The old guy?"

"Yeah."

"That's too bad. He's okay?"

"He's been unconscious for almost three weeks. It's a coma. He's all banged up, too." Hogan told him about the aquarium.

"Geez," Leon said, and then was quiet. Hogan felt bad for deflating the conversation. He wanted very much to tell Leon about Lily, but he couldn't think of any way to put it that wouldn't sound creepy or half-crazy or fully crazy.

"You seeing anyone?" Leon said, as if reading Hogan's mind. "Uh-uh."

"You still in touch with Denise?"

"No." Denise, of the yoga and floppy furniture, was the only girlfriend Hogan had had during his friendship with Leon, which had elevated her to a place of little deserved but unshakeable significance in Leon's mind.

"So work's good?" Leon finally asked.

"Sure." He tried to say about the *No Move* pile because maybe that would make a good story, but Leon said "Now you're breaking up. Can you hear me? Can you hear me?" Hogan could hear him but longed to be off the phone and free of this stilted imitation of their friendship. He made up something about having to make dinner, which he knew Leon knew was a lie, since all Hogan ever did for dinner was stick things in the microwave, but Leon either didn't hear or didn't protest.

"Good to talk to you, buddy," Leon yelled. "I hope your friend gets better." Hogan hung up without trying to explain Mr. Orachuk was not his friend; he was an old man who happened to live across the hall.

And when he died three days later, Hogan felt nothing but a numb tingling up the base of his spine. Is this shock? he wondered. Or grief? Mr. Orachuk had never regained consciousness—cardiac arrest had finally done him in—and by the time Hogan arrived at the hospital from work, the room had been stripped bare, sheets pulled tightly around the bed, chair pushed neatly into the corner.

Hogan stood in the doorway, tapping one foot. He was not sure what to do with himself. His head felt weighty on his neck. It struck him how little difference it made to the room, the removal of Mr. Orachuk from it. Hogan felt a low burbling in his chest, not unlike indigestion, and he realized he was angry. Angry that the old man had, after all of Hogan's hours next to his bed, died alone. Angry that the son had never shown up. Angry at the hospital for not calling Hogan and notifying him, even if he wasn't anybody. Angry at the Leons and the Lilys–yes, the Lilys too–of the world, who seemed to come into his life for the express purpose of rooting around in the emptiness of it. And angry at himself, for standing here now, fixed in this doorway, with no place else to go.

"He's still down in the morgue if you want to see him," said one of the nurses who had come up behind him, the one with the uneven eyes (one a good half-inch higher than the other). Donna, Hogan thought her name might be. He was embarrassed to be found this way, standing in a doorway, crying.

"Sorry," he said, and she assured him there was no need to apologize. She set a hand on his back.

"There, there," Donna the nurse said, and Hogan imagined she had a full stable of children back home, ones she tucked in each night, read picture books to, sang songs to about the moon. She told Hogan how to get to the morgue (down six floors to the basement) and gave a short speech about the importance of saying goodbye. He thought briefly about kissing her.

Alone in the elevator, he watched his reflection in the steel door. The metal was warped and murky with fingerprints, so his face was diffuse and clownish, his forehead improbably high, his red eyes stretched into alien-like orbs, his mouth and chin truncated. He looked pathetic. He even said it out loud as they passed the fifth floor: "Pathetic." It felt good to say. Between the fourth and third floor, he decided he was done. Done with Lily, done with the fantasizing. He didn't want to end up like Mr. Orachuk, festering away in his apartment for years, only to end up laid out cold on a slab in some hospital. Hogan would get on track, maybe go back to school. Away. Somewhere away from San Jose. And he would study to be something important, a businessman or a veterinarian. He'd stop listening in on other people's conversations. He would meet a nice girl, maybe someone who already had kids and was looking for someone quiet and dependable. He would get real. He liked the sound of that. It sounded like a slogan. He would be someone with a slogan. At floor two, he said "Get real," out loud, and he could feel his heartbeat, strong as a drum, beating against his sternum.

And then the elevator stopped on the first floor and the doors slid open and in came a woman who looked dully at Hogan before facing the panel of buttons and pressing B even though it was already lit, and Hogan thought he might suddenly choke on his saliva, might accidentally swallow his tongue.

It was her. He knew it. It was something almost indiscernible—the curve of her hip, the pale of her neck, the smooth of the back of her hand. Why she was dressed in plain clothes, not the orange scrubs, seemed strange to him, as was the fact that she carried only a tiny change pouch. Strange too that she wouldn't be wearing her hearing aid, but there was little time for such thoughts; there were only seconds between when the doors closed again and when they'd reach the basement.

He would say to her: "It's me. Hogan. 9109 M."

He would say: "Sometimes, I have dreams where you are touching my face."

He would say: "I just want to see what it looks like when you laugh."

He would say: "I've never been to England." He would say: "Come away with me."

The elevator came to a dull thud against the basement floor. When the doors started to slide back open, it hadn't been enough time; that's all he was thinking, not enough time. And so when she began to move, he felt the panicky rush of his life slipping away from him, a queasily familiar feeling, and the noise came from his mouth like a bullet, and his hand shot out too, so it happened all at once, his fingers grasping her shoulder, her name ringing out against the steel—and there was one quick second as she turned to him, her head whirling, her eyes wide and full of fear, her mouth twisted into a knot, before what was about to happen happened, when Hogan felt bad for startling a deaf woman but was giddy, so giddy for the story she would tell of this moment, the wild and witty and nearly unbelievable story Lily would one day tell of the moment they finally met.

lines of
communication

THE MARITAL THERAPIST SAID they need to establish new lines of communication, so Carla started making Edgar rebus puzzles. The first one was easy:

"I see you?" Edgar said at the breakfast table before he left for campus. She'd made him oats, steel cut. He said his answer after having studied the rebus puzzle for a very long time.

"Yes!" she said. "I see you, Edgar."

"Thank you," Edgar said.

I see you was incorrect, but Carla didn't have the heart. The answer was "I am inside of you" or "I am a part of you." She would have accepted either.

She'd planned to follow it with the inverse—

—which now she'd have to forgo. It was okay to forgo, she told herself. Marriage was an improvisation; it was making and remaking.

The next one, a sentence:

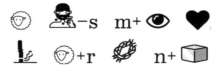

Edgar studied the rebus over dinner. Carla had made chicken tika masala, her go-to from their trip to southern India years earlier. This replaced her gazpacho, her previous go-to from their trip to Portugal years even earlier.

"Canned tomatoes?" Edgar said, pressing the back of his fork into the chicken.

She had wanted to tell him 'Ewe r knot careful' but she couldn't come up with a rebus for careful. Nice was close enough, and also true.

"We shave the sheep with a seeing heart butt?" he said after a long time. He was joking, and at his own expense, which was unusual for Edgar. His joking was usually about everyone else.

Edgar wasn't good at the rebus puzzles. Carla liked this about Edgar. Edgar was a professor of history. He was the leading scholar of pre-industrial Hungary in the world. Edgar knew more about pre-industrial Hungary than all the people of Hungary.

When the marital therapist checked in about the new lines of communication, Carla said, "Great!" She loved coming up with the rebuses. They made her brave. She wished the marital therapist had suggested this years earlier, though they hadn't had a marital therapist years earlier, the marital therapist only coming into play when the PhD student in pre-industrial Hungary (they existed? They existed!) sent the text in the middle of the night, Edgar deaf to it from behind his C-PAP machine, Carla the one to see the three words.

"Edgar?" the marital therapist said now. The marital therapist often had to say Edgar's name for Edgar to say.

"I don't," Edgar said. Edgar looked out the window. Carla turned to look. It was only a tree.

On their trip to Portugal, the boys had been so little, and Carla hadn't spoken Portuguese (still didn't). So much of the vacation had been wrangling and herding and comforting and coaxing while only having a half sense of what was happening around her, a half sense of the beautiful churches she was supposed to be admiring, a half sense of the cobblestones that Edgar kept remarking upon, and not because the boys kept tripping and scraping their knees and the pads of their palms but because the history of cobblestone in southern Europe, Edgar wanted them to know, was really a very interesting story.

One morning over scrambled egg whites (had to watch Edgar's high cholesterol), she handed him:

[rebus: eye] +m   sm+ [rebus: framed portrait]

and he knit his brow and shrugged and it occurred to her maybe he wasn't bad at rebuses. Maybe he wasn't trying. That night on his pillow she wrote him:

[rebus: sheep] +r   a   [rebus: ox] +e

He looked before giving a *ffh* and moving it off the pillow like one might an interloping katydid or a hotel dinner mint, not roughly, but clearing the way for the business of a pillow. He was not trying. It had been a test, the easiest rebus yet. Edgar was many things, but not a bully. Had he given it more than half a glance, he would have protested, Edgar exquisitely attuned to injustice toward himself. Instead, he kissed Carla on the corner of her lip and strapped himself into his C-PAP.

At the restaurant in Portugal–she remembered it exactly, tiny, dark walls, sconces, a handsome waiter with dark skin and dark hair–it was the second to last night, the boys exactly the right amount of tired and at the same time, sedate in their chairs, an event as rare and notable as an eclipse, the end of the trip near enough for Carla to be buoyed from her exhaustion and disappointment and unshakeable sense that everything was impossible and she was getting it all wrong. When the handsome waiter set down the soup, and she tasted her first taste, the gazpacho moved her in ways she didn't know she could be moved by soup. She'd never had anything like it: cold, sharp, dense, spicy, smooth. It had filled her.

Carla stopped saying anything except the rebuses to see if Edgar noticed. At breakfast:

$$\text{👁} +m \quad \text{👔} +rd$$

Two days later, before bed:

The marital therapist checked in. Carla let Edgar go first. Edgar shrugged. "I don't–"

"You don't what?" the marital therapist asked.

Edgar shrugged.

"I said lettuce fuck and he ignored me," Carla said.

"What?" Edgar said. "What are you–?"

"What disinterests you about making love to Carla?" the marital therapist asked Edgar.

"She never said!" Edgar said, exquisitely attuned. "She never!"

There'd been a crystalline moment in Portugal, Carla nearly finished with the gazpacho but not quite, she slowing to savor the last of it, even then knowing to slow down for the good things when they came, and she took in her husband and her boys in the half-lit tableau of the restaurant, half a world away from home and thought: all this for a guileless gal from Sioux Falls, who'd gone bananas for her Intro to World History TA, he so handsome and sophisticated, she so fat with his first baby before she could see the other side of sophomore year. What she felt was lucky and grateful and full.

She made him his goulash for dinner, his favorite. Edgar pronounced it gulyás, always, so many gulyáses over so many years. "Good," he proclaimed (Gulyás, if it hit Edgar at the right moment, made him expansive) "girl."

Tonight she had a single question.

Y 🌿 🐑 m+🎂−c
m+🫛−p f+〰
✋ n 🏛✓+id?

"The sheep," Edgar said. "Always with the sheep. Good to see we're letting it eat cake now. And peas. And allowing it an eel."

She'd tried with gazpacho over a number of years, well past when she understood gazpacho to be exotic or even particularly novel. For years, the issue was too much garlic and then not enough garlic, followed by a period of "vinegar" and "more vinegar" until finally, one night Edgar said "Uch," at a first, vinegary spoonful. The boys had found that funny, the noise and their father's screwed up face. They weren't so young by then, old enough to know better, but excited utterances were not like their father, displays of emotion either. Carla watched Edgar, seeing his dawning surprise. He hadn't meant to clown, but his face bloomed at the boys' reaction, tickled and pleased with himself, as if realizing for the first time these were not shrunken men at the table, but children, and his. He screwed his face even screwier. "Uch!" he said loudly. "This is terrible soup!" and the three of them laughed.

Carla had a rebus in her head for a long time. First it was:

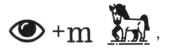

which she knew was too obscure for Edgar—or anyone. It didn't matter. It was a secret to herself. Eventually, it turned into

$$\text{👁} +m \quad d+ \text{🔫} -g$$

which Edgar could understand, were he willing. She pictured Edgar finding the rebus on the table and waiting for his breakfast and wondering what was taking so long, getting up from the table and backtracking to the bedroom to be sure she wasn't still there, hidden beneath the blankets, Edgar calling her name, peeking in half-open bathroom doors. "Carla!" he would call, a scratch to his voice, his throat always dried out in the morning from the C-PAP. She pictured Edgar returning to the table, flummoxed, picking up the paper for the first time, really studying it.

She pictured and pictured this for so long, she thought she would keep picturing it after. She thought it would become the crystalline moment of her next era, since she had no way of knowing the next era would be taken up by entirely new things—a zing of chili in her dark chocolate, a Pomeranian with an incontinence problem but such a sweet face, a dwarf bonsai she knew to keep humid from the very detailed instructions, so she spritzed and spritzed it dutifully and happily, several times a day.

don't leave me

I AM WEARING MY *Don't Leave Me* t-shirt to my blind date. We have 250 of them. Red background. Black writing, in big block letters across the front. Mel and I came up with the idea one night on the phone. She used to date a silk screener and as soon as we thought of it, she hung up with me, called him, called me back and said, *It's a go. We can do 250 for under a grand.* Mel's ex-boyfriends always stay in love with her. That's how we got the t-shirts for wholesale, less than four bucks a piece. *We can sell them*, Mel said. *We can sell them for at least ten dollars,* I said. *Fifteen*, Mel said. *Twenty-five*, I said. We're like that with each other, Mel and I, not the best of influences, no one to tether the other to the ground. We could have a talk show, we always say to each other. We would be so funny. *We would make people laugh*, Mel says. *We would make each other laugh*, I say, *fuck the other people*. It's easy, second nature, to get carried away with Mel.

The best part about the shirts, she said the next day, *is that either people will get it or they won't, either people will love it or they'll just stare at us like we're nuts. And the people willing to shell out thirty bucks for one of these, we'll know, they're one of us. We'll know,* Mel said, *us or them, us or them,* and she was bouncing up and down, twirling her hair in her finger the way she does when she gets excited, the way that's girlish and flirty and keeps men in love with her long after she dumps them and makes me think it would be so much easier if we were lesbians.

When the t-shirts were ready, the silk screener brought them to my house. Two hundred and fifty t-shirts make for some big boxes. Four of them. The silk screener and I dragged them across my hardwood floors to my back closet, bending the cardboard flaps as we tugged. He broke open the top of one box; it was so red inside, blood red, the color shocking even to me who is not easily shocked—and he pulled one out and held it to his chest and smiled. The silk screener always had a half-grown mustache like a pubescent boy. And the t-shirt seemed perfect there, below his grin, below his terrible mustache and his ruddy cheeks, and right then I knew we were onto something big, Mel and I.

The boxes sat in my closet. We hadn't thought of exactly how to sell them. Each of us had visions of a street corner stand, like newspapers or cigarettes or lemonade, but no plan. And then we got busy with other things. I fell in love and Mel got a new temp placement in the US Bank building, alphabetizing mostly. Even the simplest of tasks, she would say, becomes taxing after eight hours. She would ask me, *What comes first, M or O? V or S? J or H?* and when I paused, she would yell, *See! See! See!* The guys I fell in love with were a spastic, then a cripple. I didn't call them that at the time. Except with Mel, to make her laugh. *How's what's his name?*

she'd say about the first one, and I would tell her something he'd done that day like whip his arm to his side or yell *fargut* when we were in line at the bank. *What's fargut?* she'd ask and I'd say, *Nothing, it's imaginary, it's just some made-up thing he had to scream because he's a spastic.* And she would laugh, which was good to hear, because mostly she was angry with her stupid job and with me, the way we always got angry if the other fell in love, full of the quiet brooding of the one left behind.

The blind date is in a fancy restaurant. The maître d' cocks his head when he sees me, arching one brow and twisting his mouth into a strained smile. *I'm sorry, ma'am*, he says, you need reservations here. I give him my blind date's name. He runs his manicured finger along the list, getting a look of pinched surprise when he finds it. *Well, what do you know?* he says, looking at my blood red chest. What are you staring at? I want to say. I am a warrior. I am a warrior for love.

Satchel—that was the spastic's name—had stood in the lobby of a movie theater, grimacing, grunting, and needing to shake every person's hand as they streamed past him to the exit. I had gone to see something scary about zombies, a terrible virus, and the end of the world, and I had gone during the day on purpose to make it less frightening. And because during the day it felt more acceptable to be there by myself. Satchel had stood inside the outer doors, facing the wrong direction, the rest of us blinking into the sudden light, edgy and suspicious after two hours of gore. And there was Satchel, with his politician's handshake. Using both hands, gripping people's palms with one, clasping their elbow with the other. Running blind, a marathoner's

determination, to each person. *It's an illness*, he explained
to me later. Uncontrollable urges. Noises, movements. His
mother had gone to the bathroom, left him alone in the
lobby for just that one moment. I never told him I had at
first thought he was retarded. That I was scared and the
small part of me that wasn't scared was disgusted. How I'd
slowed as everyone tried to get away from him, tried to make
a wide berth, a sea of people separated by poor Satchel. He
followed all of them, hands outstretched, the grunting noise
truly alarming. And finally it was my turn. Satchel took my
hand and looked at me with his dopey, desperate eyes, and
I saw his panic and his helplessness, and I knew that this
was a man who would never, ever be able to hide anything.
Uncontrollable urges, I said to him a few days later, running
my hand down his sweaty chest, my tongue on his nipple,
I know a little something about those. It was a joke, a private
joke, the first in a string of them between me and Satchel,
who in the end, turned out to be a good man.

When I wasn't with Satchel, I was with Mel. She and I sat
on her couch, me flipping through TV stations, Mel painting
her toenails. She was broke and had run out of cable money
and only got seven channels now, most of them snowy or
home shopping. Mel said, *Why are you dating a spastic?* I said,
*I like him. And he's only spastic some of the time; you can never
really predict. That makes it kind of fun.* Mel said, *Well I liked
the real estate agent.* She always liked guys once I was done
dating them. *He had a lisp*, I said. Mel laughed and started
talking like Elmer Fudd: *I wuv you Aw-ih-sun. Wiw you
mawwy me?* I laughed too, even though that was nothing
like the real estate agent's lisp; he had a slight raspy sound

to his *th*'s. *I wuv you too, Meh-wah-nee*, I said. I made her do my nails when she was done with hers. *Besides*, I said, *the real estate agent dumped me, remember?* She held my toes in her hand. *What a dumbass*, she said, blowing gently to make them dry.

I get seated all the way in the back of the restaurant at a table against the far wall. I am the only one wearing a t-shirt. Everyone else is in a suit coat or a silk blouse or a sweater-jacket with a faux fur collar. Maybe it's real fur; I can't tell. Steak, they serve steak here, and the air smells charred and bloody. The waiter introduces himself as Hank and hovers, hawk-like and questioning. *Would you like a menu to peruse? Perhaps an appetizer? Some more water?* He sounds amused.

Satchel and his mother each had their own La-Z-Boy. His was blue, hers brown. Their living room smelled of plug-in air freshener; I sat on the couch while Satchel hiccupped softly in his La-Z-Boy and his mother asked me questions from hers. *What kind of work do you do? Where does your family live?* There was an oddly quaint quality to the scene, boy bringing girl home to Mom, except that Satchel had gray sideburns and a bit of a paunch and he sat strumming his fingers over his lips and clicking his tongue. *Satchel was home schooled*, his mother told me. *Satchel has many talents*, she said. *Satchel used to play the flute*, she said. I started laughing. I didn't mean to. *That's wonderful*, I said, and she showed me pictures, a whole album full, this skinny little Satchel with stooped shoulders and a full head of tangled hair. Every few pages, there was one with his face contorted or his arm jutting from his body at a bizarre angle. She didn't seem to notice. *See here? See here?* she said, pointing to each one, leaving fingerprints on the plastic coating. *Yip*, it sounded like he was saying from his La-Z-Boy, *yip yip yip yip yip.*

And I could see—with him and then later with Russ—that I was safe from harm, the one with the upper hand. It was a nice feeling, not unlike ice cream melting slowly on my tongue. I savored it.

I met Russ on TriMet. Russ on the Bus. There was a new driver that day, a shiny-faced woman with flat, greasy hair the color of straw. Russ was at a stop halfway down Hawthorne, waiting near the curb in his wheelchair. He wore black racing gloves, the kind with the tips of the fingers cut out. He had a briefcase in his lap and wore a not-so-shabby suit. A nice pinstripe. It seemed like a surprise, the suit and the briefcase and the chair together like that. Russ was causing a commotion because the new driver couldn't get the lift to work. She was worriedly pressing buttons, pulling on an antique-looking crank. The bus creaked and sighed, but it wouldn't turn its stairs into a ramp that lowered smoothly to the ground. You could see the people waiting at the stop behind Russ growing impatient, trading glances, scowling at the driver or at the back of Russ' head, which even at the time I thought was unfair, because he was only waist high.

It ended up that Russ had to be carried. *I'm sorry, I'm sorry,* the driver kept repeating, which, as the rest of us could see, was only making it worse. She folded Russ' chair and carried it up; a young woman took the briefcase, two men carried Russ, his arms draped over each of their shoulders, his legs hanging noodley and askew in the pinstripe. But his face was

the remarkable part. It was red, fire engine red, full of cartoon
rage where the steam comes out of the ears and the far-off
train engine makes a two-note whistle. His jaw was clenched,
his lips pursed. He squinted, focusing far away. When they
sat him back in his chair, he thanked no one, looked at no
one, even though people were craning their necks to stare at
him. He grabbed his briefcase back from the girl. His hands
worked just fine. When he rang the bell for his stop (I had
been watching him the whole time; what else could anyone be
expected to do?), I ran down the aisle and took the briefcase
from him, following the clumsy parade of helpers down the
stairs, standing next to Russ on the sidewalk as folks got him
adjusted in his chair. The cords of his neck were so tight, he
looked like a tortoise. The rain was starting to come, light as
spittle. *You want this?* I held the briefcase in front of me. I
had meant it to be flirty and playful. He stared at me. *This?*
I giggled, shaking it a little. He stared. I handed him the
briefcase. He started down the sidewalk, and fast; the chair
was electric and I had to jog a little to keep up. Neither of us
talked for a while, until I said, *Nice suit*, and he stared at me
again like he had forgotten I was there. Russ shook his head,
and we were in the wrong neighborhood from where I was
supposed to be, into the cute houses that looked like they'd
been Easter-egg dipped in bright colors with families inside
who had a bazillion dollars for a home. The rain was starting
to come down heavier and the sun was already sinking behind
trees and I had a horrible dread settling in me. I stopped
walking. *I think you're sexy*, I said. *At least you can give me your
phone number*, I said.

It was a bike accident, Russ told me later. *Motorcycle?* I'd said,
feeling prickles of excitement. *10-speed*, he said. He'd been

fifteen and lost control going down a hill, veered into a parked car, flipped over, and landed on his head. A tenth grader in a wheelchair. *I used to play soccer*, he said, which was the closest he came to sentimentality. He couldn't sit still. That was the funny part. He had to keep his hands moving all the time. Sometimes he lifted free-weights. Sometimes he folded pieces of paper or napkins into these little boxes, his one origami trick. Sometimes he drew funny caricatures, like the one of me with my nose too big and my chin too long that hurt my feelings even though I didn't say so. Mostly he knitted.

I couldn't stand the knitting. There was something so disconcerting about the skeins of yarn and the bobbing needles and the half-finished scarf or sweater trailing off Russ' lap down the side of his chair. It made him look dainty. Feminine. He didn't care. It's relaxing, he said. It's Zen. I started making jokes. *Granny, how's the sweater going?* I would say. *I could get you a subscription to* Ladies' Home Journal; *I hear they have some lovely patterns in there.* He ignored me mostly, his fingers moving so quickly, like he was playing a piano concerto in his lap. He made me a hat with a pompom and ear flaps. It was a ridiculous hat; the pompom was orange. He laughed when he handed it to me and I tried to find it amusing, but the whole thing was getting to me. He was at it all the time unless we were eating or sleeping or having sex. And yes, we could have sex. That still worked, though he insisted we do it under blankets, saying he didn't want to get cold, but I knew it was that he was embarrassed by the atrophied muscles, the shriveled skin against his stick figure limbs, which I stared at while he slept, poking lightly with my fingernails, finding myself fascinated in the way I used to be fascinated by centipedes or slugs as a kid.

He started an afghan, each square a pink and purple flower. Whenever I saw him pulling the yarn from his yarn box, a big plastic storage crate with a rainbow assortment of skeins, my stomach knotted. The clack clack of the needles made my jaw clench and I found myself wanting to grab something and shake it mercilessly. I asked him how many squares total. He said *64* and I laughed out loud and said, *No way, no way*, and he stared at me. I told him he needed to quit the knitting while I was over. He asked why. I told him it bothered me. He told me I was being crazy. I told him he was being stubborn. He said, *I'm not some gimp you can order around.* I knew the argument had gone bad, but I didn't know how to find a way back and looking at his mouth, the tight line of his lips, the quiver of his jaw, I knew he didn't either. And it was almost funny, except not, so I said, *It's me or the quilt*, and even then, I thought somehow we'd be able to get out of this, one of us saying uncle or chicken or sorry.

I am watching the front of the restaurant, following the path of the maître d' as he seats a young couple, then a trio of women in black dresses. He returns each time to his podium by the front door, pulling on the back of his suit coat, straightening his shoulders. He seats a middle-aged couple and their two children, staring at me each time he comes into the dining room, as if he is surprised I am still here, surprised I haven't stolen the silver napkin ring and escaped through the kitchen.

Good riddance to bad rubbish, Mel said about Russ. She was sitting on my bed, flicking my nose, trying to make me laugh. *Quit it*, I said. She pretended to poke me in the eye. *Doink*, she said, as she brought her finger to my eyeball. Her breath smelled like pepperoni from the pizza she'd brought me. I'd eaten half a slice. She'd had four. *Doink*, she kept saying, pointing at my eye. *Doink. Doink. Shut up*, I finally said, then: *Tickle my arm*. She ran her fingernails up and down my skin. *I'm sad*, I said. *I know*, she said. We were quiet for a while until she said *He was a dick*. I laughed. *How would you know?* I said. *You never even met him*. One of her nails was torn and it was scratchier than the rest. She said, *I'm assuming he's a dick if he dumped you*. I'd liked the way Russ would cook me stir-fried vegetables and read me articles from *The Economist* about arcane countries I'd barely heard of and wake me in the mornings by kissing my back. *Doink, doink, doink*, Mel said. It was so stupid; I tried not to laugh, but I couldn't help it. *You are fucking annoying*, I said. *Doink, doink, doink*, she said, bobbing her head up and down, grinning idiotically, sticking her tongue out of the side of her mouth. *Keep tickling*, I said. She did.

With Satchel, the problem hadn't been me so much as my friends, the loose knot of people Mel and I had known since college. We are a stoic, mean bunch, not spiteful as much as lazy, finding a certain comfort in our well-worn cruelty— making fun of Don's beer belly or Lois' tiny breasts and nasal voice, Mel's perpetual unemployment, my sluttiness. Satchel sat next to me at the end of the horseshoe booth, making barking noises, whistling, whipping his arm to his side every so often. We were on our second or third round and Don was talking about his bitch of a boss, who gave him the shittiest of the projects and called him on weekends to ask why he wasn't working to meet the latest deadline. Every time Satchel made noise, Don would stop and stare, and I'd say "Don," but not anything else and Satchel would look at his gin and tonic, rolling the glass between his palms, trying to sit still. I could feel his leg against mine, shaking with the effort, and I put a hand on it. I did. The longer Don stared, the worse it got, and Satchel would end up yelling something like *Cripenut* or *Sunburn*, which would make everyone laugh, which would make Satchel whip his arm out to his side. It was ugly. I tried, but I couldn't pick a side. I was embarrassed for Satchel. Embarrassed for my friends. Again and again, I made Satchel go back, hoping things would straighten themselves out, that he would stop twitching or they would be nice or both, because I felt entitled to this much at least, to be out with my boyfriend and my friends having some drinks, having some fun. During the ride home every time, Satchel was silent, as silent as he could be. *That was nice when Lois asked you about your job*, I would say. *That was good when Mel shared her mozzarella sticks. Are you okay?* I would say. *Are you okay? Are you okay?* all the way home. *Sure*, he would finally say when he dropped me at my apartment, *What could be wrong? Great. Peachy. Peachy fucking keen.* And when he was angry, he was still, no movement at all, his fists clenched at his temples and his eyes wide and accusing, staring right at me, waiting for me to apologize or explain or do something other than just sit there, or open the car door and leave, which is what I eventually did.

I didn't even think about the t-shirts until it fell apart with both of them. Two hundred and fifty, ready to wear. It was convenient; I could just throw the dirty one on the floor at the end of the day, pick out a clean one in the morning. The first time, I left my house, no sweater, no jacket, even though it was cool out, and I walked. People stared. A woman in a business suit looked at my chest and then my face, her eyes beady and humorless. I held my shoulders back, chin forward, remembering those commercials from when we were younger, with the girl and the book on her head, walking in trance-like lines, back and forth along her carpeting. *You too can be a model.* I was cold; my nipples poked against the shirt, the material itchy and stiff. I felt bold and mostly unashamed. I crossed the Morrison Bridge, the wind in my face, the river choppy and gray. A barge moved slowly through the water, barely looking like it was moving. Downtown, I marched through the bus mall, looking full of purpose with my quick strides and my eyes focused on the distance. By the time I made it to Mel's apartment—a one-bedroom above a cigar bar, her place always smelling smoky and ashen—my nose was running and I couldn't warm my hands, even in my pockets. She screamed when she opened the door and saw me there, in my red and black shirt. Jumped up and down and pointed, laughing, laughing, laughing. *Holy shit holy shit holy motherfucking shit*, she said. And I could see from her face that she'd forgotten all about this, that in the months since the boxes were delivered, the whole thing had flitted out of her head, and now I was a revelation, a birthday present, a girl jumping out of a cake. *It's brilliant*, she said. *We're brilliant.* Her hands were over her mouth. It was her Miss-America-just-been-crowned look. *How many months is 250 days?* I asked. *More than eight*, she said. *I don't have to do wash for more than eight months*, I said. *Except for your pants*, Mel said, still laughing. Except for my pants.

Hank has filled my water glass three times and brought me a vodka martini with a lemon twist. Thin trails of perspiration roll down the sides of the glass. We had agreed on seven, my blind date and I. It is seven fifteen. Seven sixteen now.

Mel met someone at the alphabetizing job. *A suit*, she said, and she tried to be dismissive, telling me about his pointy nose and the slightly sour smell of his breath. But his name kept coming up in conversation. Mitch. He was a banker of some sort. She wasn't sure exactly what he did, but his office was in the corner, with windows on both walls and a secretary who sat at a desk outside his door. *He has a goddamned secretary all for himself*, she said. *How many people can you name with a secretary all to himself?* I couldn't name one. Soon they were having lunch a few times a week and then every day and then one afternoon he met her for her break, and they slipped down into the underground parking garage and had sex in the back seat of his Beemer. That's what she called it, a Beemer. She said the smell of sex and sweat and leather made her realize why so many people were into bondage. He took her places like a spoken word concert at the Schnitz and a benefit dinner for the Portland symphony and a lecture at PSU on the Global Economy and Central America. I said, *Was it as boring as it sounds?* And she said, *No*, quickly and loudly, like she was surprised I'd even asked. I found it suspect that a banker with a corner office was dating a temp alphabetizer, but I didn't mention that to Mel, because there's no talking to her when she's in love.

I saw Russ on the number 14 bus twice. The first time, I watched him from my seat in the back, waiting for him to leave before I rang the bell, missing my stop by half a mile. The second time I said, *Hello*, and he said, *Hello*, and we were strangers again and I thought how time doesn't heal all wounds, time is more like a Vicodin or Percoset where you can still feel the pain but you don't care so much anymore because it's shoved somewhere beneath a hazy layer of numbness and exhaustion.

I took to wearing the stupid earflap hat to bed. It was scratchy and too tight around my forehead, but I liked how it muffled noise just the tiniest bit and how it made the part of me that stuck out from the blanket feel less exposed.

Mel started saying *de facto*. She called Lois and Bob our *de facto* friends. She referred to her TV as a *de facto* means of diversion. *What?* I said. She repeated *de facto means of diversion.* I told her she got that from Mitch and she told me I was being stupid. *Either you got it from him or it's a strange sort of coincidence*, I said. *A de facto coincidence.*

I called Satchel; his mother answered. When I said, *This is Allison*, she didn't respond. *Allison Stone*, I said. *Satchel is not home*, she said and I didn't believe her but I didn't fight it either.

I called Satchel, I told Mel while I was flipping through her channels. She sighed and didn't answer. She was lying on the couch, her arm draped over her face, like she was sick or dying. *What's wrong?* I said. *Nothing*, she said. I found ice skating on one channel, the picture distorting into jagged zigzags every couple of seconds. *That guy is definitely gay*, I said. Mel looked at the screen. *Yeah*, she said, but hardly. When her phone rang, she ran to get it and it was obvious who it was from the way she was giggling and the way she went into the bedroom and closed the door behind her.

Mitchell, I heard her call him. And *Mr. Man.* And even once, *Lovey.*

I started having lunch dates with Lois, where she smacked her lips on the pad thai and bitched a lot about her neighbor's dog. One night I made Betty Crocker cake for dinner. I called Mel while I was whipping up the soupy batter—it was pink cake with confetti frosting; I knew she'd appreciate that—but she wasn't home.

I need to pee, but I don't want to get up to use the restroom. The woman at the next table is sawing through her steak, the knife screeching against her plate, the meat bleeding in oily pinkish ribbons. The man chews loudly. They don't speak— they're both concentrating—but beneath the table, his legs are stretched toward hers and their feet—her suede pumps, his black dress shoes—look like shoes thrown onto the floor of the closet, lazily intertwined.

Mitch has a friend, Mel said one night on the phone. *He's a real nice guy who just got divorced. A tax attorney. And he's ambulatory.* She laughed. I didn't. *Maybe you want to meet him*, she said, *maybe go for drinks.* I told her I didn't think so. She sighed loudly and said, *I liked it when you dated regular guys. Like the one studying to be a chiropractor*, she said, *remember him?* Of course I remembered him. *Well how about it, then?* Mel said. I didn't answer, and I could hear her breath getting raspy and loud, the way it does when she's annoyed. *I remember when you weren't so cynical*, she finally said. Mel never talked to me like this. My cheeks burned and my breath was hot and chalky against the phone. This was the worst part of Mel in love—high, mighty, holier than.

Please, she said to me one night, her fingertips pressed to her lips in a prayer position. *Just one date.* She looked like she could cry, honest to god. We were sitting on my bed and it had been so long since she'd been over to my place, I just wanted to do something like braid her hair. *Can I braid your hair?* I said. *Only if you answer me first*, she said. *Okay*, I said. *Lay off already. I'll go. I'll meet him*, and she bounced up and down on her knees, like my bed was a trampoline, clapping her hands and saying, *Yay! Yay! Yay!* It was depressing, how excited she was. Stop it, I said. Stop it. But she wouldn't stop jumping and, to be honest, it made her look foolish, made her look like a monkey.

She finally brought Mitch to drinks. *M and M*, I said when he sat down and introduced himself, a handshake for everyone, one at a time around the circle, as if this were a job interview. *Heard a lot about you*, he said to me. His handshake was firm, vigorous, embarrassing. *M and M*, I said again because no one had responded the first time. Mel turned sideways in the booth so her whole body was facing Mitch, her hand resting on his shoulder the entire time. Whenever the conversation veered into one of our stupid, familiar places (Lois' neighbor veered off their shared driveway onto Lois' lawn, leaving a deep muddy rut in her grass. Was it an accident? A spiteful act?), Mel would chirp up with a fact about Mitch. Did you know he was the cockswain on his crew team in college? That he ran the Portland Marathon last year? I made a cockswain joke. Mel ignored me. Everyone was charmed by Mitch because he wore a nice suit and made allusions to Marx, which no one expected and no one understood. *Are you married?* I said. He stared at me. Mel stared at me. *No*, Mitch said. *Have you ever been married?* I asked. *Yes*, Mitch said. *I thought so*, I said. *You thought so?* he said. He was smiling. Mel was not. *Sure*, I said, and I ran my hand across the top of my own head, in the exact spot where his hair was thinning. *What happened?* I said and he laughed. *That's a long story*, he said. *We have time*, I said, looking to Lois and Don for encouragement. Lois was stirring her drink. Don was smiling, open mouthed, staring from Mitch to Mel to me and then back again. *Well?* I said. *We're among friends here, Mitch.* Mel's hand squeezed his shoulder. *Once or more than once?* I said. *I mean, have you been married a couple of times?* When he didn't answer, I said, *More than a couple? Three? Four?* Don held his hand over my beer glass. *Maybe you've had enough there, kiddo*, he said. Mel was shaking her head, stroking Mitch's arm. *Maybe*, I said. *Maybe not.* I was incapable of quiet. Lois asked Mitch how long he'd been at the bank. He answered. I wasn't listening. She complained to him that the bounced check fees were too high. He laughed and said that wasn't his department, but he'd see what he could do. Mel wouldn't look at me, even when we all stood to leave and Mitch shook my hand again and lied and lied and lied, saying it was nice to meet me, we'd have to do it again, and the pleasure was all his.

Mel didn't call. I got it. On day one and day two, I understood. She was wronged; I was wrong. But then it grew irritating, unnerving, unforeseen. How many days would stretch between us? Was she lying pretzeled with Mitch, making careless jokes at my expense? Did her phone still work? Did mine? Where did she get this willpower? What was she doing right this minute? This minute? This? Thi–?

Another drink? Hank asks. The only thing left in my martini glass is a dime sized ring of vodka. *No thanks*, I say. *Sure you don't need anything to tide you over?* Hank asks. *A breadbasket? Even a small appetizer?* No, Hank, no. For the love of God, Hank.

When I finally called Mel—day eight—she was short with me. *What?* she said. *Stop it,* I said. *I was drunk and stupid.* When she stayed quiet, I told her about my phone call with the tax attorney, how we were going out this Friday, how he had suggested the Chart House. *What's he thinking?* I said. *The Chart House is like stupid shi-shi and not even cool.* Mel said: *What do you mean, stupid shi-shi?* She said it like she had no idea how I'd learned to talk that way. *I mean,* I said, *who goes to the Chart House?* She told me: *Decent people do. Professionals.* Her voice was slick and assured, full of confidence.

I was laughing the next time I called her, laughing already when she picked up the phone, so she'd know all was well. *I'm gonna wear the shirt,* I said. *I'm gonna wear it to the date.* Mel was quiet. I was tired of Mel being quiet. *Don't,* she finally said. *Why not?* I said. *Because he's a good guy,* she said. *You love the shirt,* I said. *The joke is old,* Mel said. *I'll wear the shirt if I want to,* I said. *It's a mistake,* she said. *Oh, you're all of a sudden the expert in the rules of courtship,* I said. And Mel took a breath into the phone. *Suit yourself,* she said and hung up first.

The maître d' pulls on the back of his jacket and leans forward at his podium, speaking to someone new. When he turns around, he looks straight at me, smiling, though not nicely, his lip curled like a magician who just got one over on us and good: lady sawed in half or put into a box and disappeared. There's the tax attorney behind him. He looks like the picture he sent—receding hairline, goatee, ears—though a picture isn't a person. A person is red-cheeked and scanning the tables for me, smiling, even if the smile is a little painted on, a little pained. I am minding my face so it doesn't look painted on, though minding my face makes me too aware of it, a trap I don't know my way out of. The picture I sent was me laughing on a coast weekend with Mel, the sunset behind me, my hair whirling in the wind, an ad for hair dye if the hair dye were for people drunk on afternoon wine and with sand in their teeth. The tax attorney is taller than I thought, a paunch where his short-sleeved dress shirt is tucked in. He stumbles behind the maître d', foot caught on foot, and he makes a low, girlish noise—*oof*—and I am mortified for him and glad for me and sad for me and sad for him and this is when he finally scans my table, me distracted from minding my face long enough that I am maybe smiling, though maybe about to cry.

Sorry, he says when he sits. *Sorry, sorry sorry. My rotty is sick. He won't stop vomiting. I don't even—*. He puts his hands in his air. Maybe he notices my shirt. Impossible to say with all his apologizing and hand waving and furling his napkin into his lap. I didn't know he had a Rottweiler. I don't know anything about him besides tax attorney and the short-sleeve dress shirt making him look like a schoolboy or a Mormon. *A Rottweiler*, I say. *Blackie*, he says, and it seems like a dumb name and possibly racist but maybe it's the kind of dog that once you meet all is forgiven. *A him dog or a her dog?* I ask as if I am new to language. *A him*, he tells me and maybe he's noticing the shirt; no, he's definitely noticing. His chin curdles the slightest curdle, and the two lines between his brows deepen, like we're nearing midnight on April 14th. He grabs his water and drinks and drinks, and even when he's out of water, he won't make eye contact. I try to remember what

I'd been hoping for but all I remember is there is nothing stupider than hope. I don't know anything about Rottweilers, and I wish there was a sunset behind me. I think of how happy Hank will be the next time he comes by, an empty water glass to fill. Hank lives for this shit. *Like a pit bull?* I say and he tells me that's a common misconception, but Blackie is a real lover. Maybe the tax attorney's smile isn't painted on, maybe that's just how he looks. *No better good boy*, he says, and maybe that's his face.

pipelines are pipes

SHELDON IS THINKING about how the heat is a punch to the teeth, which he always knows to anticipate but never fully can, the way a body refuses to remember. It is a heat that hurts his gums. He is thinking about how he originally looked up Chip Johnson from B-school to ask about sweat lodges and the name on Chip's faculty webpage was C. Ahanu Johnson and he was wearing what Sheldon could only think of at the time as a dashiki though dashiki wasn't the right word; dashiki was for Black people. What was the native word for dashiki? The shirt was a whole deal. A whole Indian deal, and not how Chip had dressed in grad school, Chip in cheap JC Penney shirts, sweat staining his collars, trying too hard till he stopped trying, a cheap door on cinderblocks for a coffee table at Chip's apartment, hollow, four sunken rectangular panels where the coke they sniffed got caught in the molding and they used all manner of fingernail, pocketknife, fork tine to dislodge. Sheldon is thinking about how he judged the native dashiki and the

C. Ahanu even if Sheldon hadn't been Sheldon for years now, Brennan Vivant, an invention of his first agent and first publicist together in a New York City whiskey bar with Sheldon, who at the time had been new to New York City and whiskey bars and book publishing. Sheldon Mendelson, they told him, did not instill the same kind of confidence as Brennan Vivant, and Sheldon had no reason to disbelieve them, in fact found believing them more intoxicating than the whiskey (and it was the best whiskey he'd ever had), Sheldon as poor and desperate as Chip in grad school but smart enough to dig himself a hole of credit card debt to at least look the part.

Veronica is thinking about how it is very very very hot in here, though of course she understands the heat to be the point. She is not an idiot, though the reasons people assume her to be are many and varied: her larger than average breasts, her (dyed) blonde hair, her southern accent, her big-mouthed husband and his abundance of money and therefore her abundance of money, her willingness to spend three thousand four hundred and ninety nine dollars plus lodging for a Bon Vivant Seminar and Self-Success weekend, her wont for taking Brennan Vivant speeches back home and repeating them to her book group ladies and her charter school fundraising committee ladies and her museum board ladies and her loud-mouthed husband: "No way to your dreams except building a pipeline to them. But have you ever thought about pipelines? Pipelines are pipes. You ever think about pipes? Pipe cleaners needed to be *invented* to clean pipes. Pipes are so filthy, no existing tool could get all the dirt out. Dirt gets a bad rap, but the world is made of dirt. So then what's your job? Your job is to get dirty in service of your dreams. Measure yourself in how dirty your hands are, not how clean."

Gilbert is thinking about how the girl next to him took off her shirt. Even in the dark he can see the outline of sweaty slopes of breasts. He can't stop looking though it feels like his eyelids are drying out from the intensity of the air. He should close his eyes and focus on breathing. Instead he's watching the girl's slick shiny boobs heave up and down with her breathing. It is impossible to get physically aroused in here, not with the feeling like they're inside a convection oven, but if he could get physically aroused he surely would, which reminds him of the cum stains on his sheets which he is embarrassed of vis a vis the cute Spanish-speaking maid on his hallway. He had not masturbated since his mom died, though now it's the third day in a row with cum stains on his sheets. He hadn't anticipated how horny Brennan Vivant would make him. He felt like he could fuck anything: a hat box, a coat hanger, a bathtub, travel shampoo. Not that Gilbert was gay, or at least not that he was aware of being gay, Gilbert open to the possibility though very very attracted to the penetrative quality of man and woman sex, the squeeze of a good, tight pussy, the sounds that came out of a woman's mouth as he fucked her soft then hard then soft again then hard, the forceful, heated breathing, the high-voiced moans, which is not all that different now from the shirtless woman next to him, and several other women around the circle—and men too, if he's not mistaken. It has the aural quality of an orgy in here. He could be inside a porno, and Gilbert is full of grief—real grief—that the heat is foreclosing on the possibility of a boner. The heat makes it feel like he'll never have a boner again.

Bette is thinking about how the air in her throat is physical, a sweat sock of heat or maybe a coffee filter of heat, which she has to breathe through, an extra step in an automatic bodily process that she never normally thinks about, but which maybe is the point, though Brennan Vivant always talks of the folly of "the point" and how focusing on "the point" takes us out of our bodies, so Bette tries only to think about bodies, which makes her think about her granddaughter, Lee, whose seizures at the start looked only like quickly blinking in one eye, though Tru, her daughter with her nursing degree and her ICU hospital job knowing immediately, Tru shrill and hysterical in her knowing, Tru having always been the kind of child who wielded her knowing like a weapon, though Tru had not been Tru as a child, Tru once having had a different name, which Tru has asked and asked and asked Bette to stop saying, though Bette is making an honest mistake, an inevitable mistake, for which she thought Tru ought to cut her some slack, though Tru was not the type for slack cutting. When Tru threatened to bar Bette from her home if Bette continued to say the old name and the old he (an even honester and inevitabler mistake), Bette knew she could not stand on principle so Bette took to standing in the mirror instead for a good twenty minutes before going over to see Tru and Tru's wife Stacia, and Tru's dying daughter, Lee, watching her own face and saying: "Tru. She. Tru. She. Tru. She. She. She. She. She. Tru. Tru. Tru. Tru. She. She. She. She. She. She. She. Tru."

Edie is thinking about how she'd like to take off her pants too. She can't stand the heat of her leggings, the sweat trapped

inside like the fabric is fusing to her. She stinks so bad–
period stink between her legs, spicy stink from her pits or
other people's pits and their cheesy crotch grease. How can
people even stand to be people, is what she's thinking. It's so
so gross, and one more reason why her German shorthaired
pointer, Beau, who she got in the divorce, thank fuck, was
at the very top of her Big Loves list from day two of the
Seminar of Self-Success weekend, which all the returnees
called *three ess weekend*, and which Edie was going to try to
be, a returnee, as soon as she got her next big OnlyFans check,
best job she ever had, easy money, the easiest, dressed up all
by herself (undressed all by herself!), never having to smell
any of her customers, her customers nothing but concepts,
avatars, fucking money. Putting Beau at the top of her Big
Loves list had made her feel badass and ashamed all at once,
like everything made her feel badass and ashamed all at once,
till it was its own feeling, self-hating pride. But then Brennan
Vivant yelled from the stage: *How many of you have a non-
human at the top of your Big Loves list?* And all around Edie
hands went up, and her hand went up, and Brennan Vivant
yelled *Happens every time* and everyone roared with laughter
including Edie.

Sheldon is thinking how the dark ridges of bodies, the
collective panting, the crush of the heat and the heavy
movements of trying, this is his favorite part, the best worst
part of the weekend, the impossible made possible, it never
not shocking him how they followed him in here. It didn't
puff him up with power, it humbled him. That's what Chip
Johnson said sweat was for, a humbling, Chip explaining this
after first saying in the phone: "Holy shit, man. Lulululululu!"
The high-pitched noise had taken Sheldon aback. Chip

had been quiet in grad school. Dumb jokes about the women he'd like to–but never would–sleep with. "I've been emailing you for years. Got all your books. I saw your HBO thing."

Sheldon explained about his assistant, and his assistant's assistants. The tidal wave of email. "A literal," Sheldon had said. "Tidal wave. You're C. Ahanu now?"

"C. Ahanu," Chip Johnson said, correcting Sheldon's pronunciation. And: "I still call you Sheldon."

Chip wasn't asking, and Sheldon at the time had mostly thought of himself as Sheldon, Brennan his pen name or his pen person, Brennan the blown-up version of himself, Sheldon pushed to the absolute extreme of his Sheldon-ness, but still Sheldon.

Chip Johnson said sweats were akin to religious ceremony. No, he'd never hallucinated. Yes, hot rocks. No, not like a sauna. You go in and out and in and out.

"It's not an extreme sport," Chip Johnson had said when Sheldon asked what would happen if you stay inside instead of going in and out and in and out. "You're thinking?" Chip Johnson said. "Of doing?"

"No, no," Sheldon told him and Chip Johnson said about colonization. He said about mascots. He said everyone's favorite Indian is a dead Indian.

"What?" Sheldon had said. That's not what he was saying at all. He was calling in order to be respectful. He was calling in order to get it right. Chip Johnson was what happened when you scrapped and scrapped and scrapped and scrapped and finally got somewhere, Sheldon thought at the time, Chip Johnson sitting upon a righteous perch.

Veronica is thinking about lobsters, specifically the long-ago time she and Dex had them shipped in a crate from the east coast so Dex could boil them on the stove. Veronica was the lobster now. She could feel her kidneys or maybe her spleen liquefying inside her.

Dex's daughter had been hysterical, crying and yelling and running in and out of the kitchen as the lobsters' pincers clacked against the insides of the stock pot. Dex rarely stood in front of his own stove. It was like seeing a moose at an armoire, and early enough in their courtship to be intoxicating, a direct line from Dex to Veronica's pelvis, everything foreplay.

"Murderers!" Dex's daughter yelled with real tears. She was covering her ears, mucus coming from one nostril. "They're going to scream!"

The thing Veronica had loved least about Dex in the beginning was his daughter. Dex's daughter was in the in-between stage of girlhood: no longer cute, not yet her own person. She was stringy and breastless and represented all the parts of Dex Veronica had no access to: his first wife, a tiny and gorgeous redhead from a wealthy family (natural gas); children.

When the lobsters had sat in their crate, Dex told Veronica to lift the first lobster out, lift the second, Dex liking to tell Veronica what to do, Veronica liking being told (in the beginning). The lobsters were the wrong color, dark like scorpions, and wriggling. Veronica hadn't anticipated the wriggling. Was it that she'd imagined them sedated or half dead? No, she hadn't imagined them at all, life with Dex not about imagining, life with Dex about riding the surreal wave (candelabra, household staff to clean the candelabra). Life with Dex was the running story Veronica told herself about life with Dex: *We're having dinner shipped in live from Massachusetts.*

The thought of them is heartbreaking now. She'd been scared the daughter was telling the truth. She'd been scared they'd scream. Someone was making a noise like a lobster now. Someone was making a noise. Someone was her.

Gilbert is thinking he is nauseous. Everything is swimming and he can't tell if the nausea is a headache or his headache is the heat or what. The topless girl has leaned so far forward, he can no longer see her or her glistening breasts in the darkness. He closes his eyes to help with the headache though it only causes more problems. Without sight, the crush of heat is even crushier; is someone crying? It sounds like a baby. They couldn't have let a baby in here.

His stomach roils. He can taste his hotel coffee up the back of his throat, his breakfast hash browns. He is suddenly too damn tired to open his eyes, even though the dark insides of his eyeballs make anything seems possible. It is very different than the collective feeling in the *Timber Room–East*, where they had so potently gathered for the past two and a half days, Gilbert here on a lark after the combination of his mom's death, his modest inheritance, and a Brennan Vivant late night special on HBO. To have found himself in a room full of people, all excited, all enraptured, all focused on one thing together, so full of want and so shameless in that want, Gilbert realized this must have been what it was like for his mother in her church. His shitty, drunk father had been a godless man, and it was the path of least resistance to that same skepticism, choosing to see his mom as silly and weak.

Gilbert, though, in *Timber Room–East* found himself stunned silly by the feeling of being surrounded and enveloped and at one with everyone, a feeling that began to ebb as soon as he was in the elevator or past the pretty

Spanish-speaking maid in the hallway or into his hotel room, until he grabbed his dick in his hand to get himself revved back up and recapture the–what? He couldn't think of the word for it, didn't know if there even was a word for it, could only think of the word for the opposite, a word he never said to himself, never needed to say to himself, because it was ever-present like his skin or his eyelids or the air he breathed so it need not be named: lonely.

Bette is thinking about how her throat is actually closing with the heat, she feels the passage growing smaller and smaller with each breath, which is unbearable though of course bearable because she is bearing it, and two (or three?) people away from her a man is heaving. She does not see the heaving in the deep dark, but she hears it and feels the bodies between her and the man (is it a man? It strikes her as masculine heaving) shifting toward and away. She waits for Brennan Vivant to do something. She thinks about what he told them as he ushered them into the sweat lodge that from the outside looked silly on the side lawn of the Ramada Inn and Suites, the humming HVAC systems exposed nearby on the indoor pool and spa's rooftop. She'd waited years—and then all weekend—for the sweat lodge. It was legendary. The breathless stories on Instagram. The viral Facebook posts.

Come inside, Brennan Vivant had said as he'd ushered them, stooping, into the tented cave, *and stay inside to die your best deaths and let go of what of what needs let going.* If Bette had been off put by *die your best death*—it brought to mind her granddaughter Lee's eyebrowless face and bald head and emaciation like those children from the terrible UNICEF commercials—she was then charmed by *let going.* Tru's wife, Stacia, was a professor of linguistics and wrote books that

Bette did not understand. Stacia loved talking about "queering the language." Stacia would like *let going* and so Tru would like *let going* and so Bette liked *let going*.

The man began retching, the noise thick and watery. Attention stilled around him, though still no Brennan. And then the man vomited, good god, the air immediately pungent with sweet sick, like Lee's sick, like Tru's sick long ago, a child with a weak stomach, when Tru was not yet Tru but instead crying over a toilet bowl, Bette rubbing her–Her!–back, thinking a child prone to unidentifiable illness a terrible fate.

Edie is thinking about not throwing up after the guy next to her threw up. She was down in rabbit pose trying to get below the heat when he puked and it splattered on her cheek and she bolted upright. The guy is trying to say something to her, but she isn't trying to listen. She is trying to get the puke off her face and trying to breathe. Someone else—not the guy next to her—is moaning a hoarse scream of a moan, a terrible noise, and she waits for Brennan Vivant to say one of his things, any of his things—*dig deep, find the pain past the pain, get to the place of your stillest heart, sink into yourself*—but he's not saying anything.

The puking guy touches her arm and she flinches. She says "Gwarp!" which isn't what she meant to say but the heat is fucking with her and *Gwarp* means both *get off me* and *Brennan Vivant, aren't you gonna do something about the puking and the screaming moans?*

She tries to breathe only through her mouth. Her mind goes to her German shorthaired pointer, Beau, because Beau is the place of her stillest heart, though she tries not to think about Tony, her pothead nephew who's dog sitting and will eat all of Edie's cereal and drain her liquor cabinet and she hopes hopes hopes keeps Beau on lead and doesn't try to act cool if some hot girl is coming in the opposite direction, doesn't let Beau off lead to run up to the girl for a meet fucking cute because Beau won't run up to the girl, he'll chase some squirrel on the other side of the street, darting into traffic, and goddamn, Edie can't bear even the thought of it, breathing the burning stink of puke down her throat, barely breathing. Beau!

Sheldon is thinking of one plus two is three plus four is seven. There always comes a point in the sweat lodge when he does numbers and it is the point at which the heat is suffocating and the smell is unbearable and people are crying and screaming and vomiting and still they do not leave. Even Chip Johnson would be impressed in spite of himself. It is never not remarkable to Sheldon that people do not leave even if he knows they will not leave because every single time they do not leave, though he wouldn't believe it unless he were here to witness their suffering. He is suffering too but his suffering is different because he has been to the end of this many times, and he will be the one to call it. They are suffering because of him. They are suffering *for* him. The only thing holding them here is their belief in Brennan Vivant. It is a belief beyond reason, beyond Sheldon's wildest imaginings.

Plus five is twelve. Plus six is eighteen. The counting is the same counting he used to do in bed as a very little boy, when it was dark and the house was still and his parents were asleep and he was alone in the dark with the monsters and the ghouls. No matter how many books he writes (eleven, the twelfth in galleys, the backlist recently reissued to have matching covers with the front: his face and the sun in various states of rising and setting), this remains his best and most

reliable meditative strategy—*plus seven is twenty-five*—and he
has never once written about it. He has kept it for himself, one
of the few things. His house has been in *Architectural Digest*.
He had been on *Oprah*—many times—when *Oprah* was still
daily, he and his (now ex-) husband on *Ellen* "to set the record
straight" about Brennan and a certain Scientologist movie
star. Their two Persians had been featured with Brennan
post-divorce, the three snuggled on the loveseat, in *People's*
recent "Stars and Their Pets." It matters to Sheldon to have
a secret (aside from the Scientologist movie star). Plus eight
is twenty-six. Plus nine is thirty-five.

Veronica is thinking she is thinking what is she thinking?
Her neck hurts from the lobster noises or it's her throat that
hurts but also it's hard to keep body parts straight. The insides
of her nostrils are singed from breathing and what the fuck?
Dex would not like what the fuck, Dex would tell Veronica
that is not how a real person speaks, as if Veronica were
pretend before she met Dex, which maybe she was. Now she's
crying though she can't say why except for everything, and
her hair is pasted to her neck. The girls on either side of her
are crying too and one of them is rocking back and forth and
it's so goddamn dark in here. She does keep catching sight of
one tiny, tiny slit of daylight, which appears and disappears
depending on how bodies shift and sway. She assumes it's the
bottom of the opening Brennan ushered them through at the
start (An hour and a half ago? Seven minutes ago?), telling
them hell is in their imagination and they were about to get
free from all known bounds of man. She feels like she can
get through this if she can see the tiny slit of light, the tiny
slit of light all she needs even though Brennan Vivant would
tell her she is closest to her own mortality when she measures

her life in need, which makes her cry even more, from not understanding what that means. Mucus drips onto her lips like when she was a girl and knew how to cry shamelessly, unafraid to suck up her own snot.

Gilbert is thinking he needs a glass of water though the thought of a glass of water makes him feel sick and he is thinking *please no not again* as his stomach lurches and the queasiness grips his throat. He's already covered in his sick. It's on his legs and in his goatee. His life is only suffocating nausea and the cramping in his side. He is thinking *please no* and he is remembering his dead mother and the cool, wet washcloth she would hold on his forehead. How she would take the thermometer from under his tongue and look at the mercury. "Oh Gil," she would say, the back of her hand on his hot cheek. "My poor Gil." He is thinking: *Mommy.*

Bette is thinking don't let her die in here. She can't die before her granddaughter, Lee, she thinks without thinking. The wrongness of this thought–the terrible, backward wrongness– seizes her almost immediately. She wishes she could take the thought back, but time only moves in one direction and the pain in her gut is like stabbing and she howls. She howls for Lee and for Tru and for Stacia and for ___ who Tru used to be but is not anymore, and the gall of Bette, the gall of herself, she thinks, of her terrible, stupid, selfish goddamned self for mourning a child who is here and hers and whole, and still it's all her terrible, stupid, selfish, goddamned self knows to do.

Edie is thinking she is going to stand up. Edie is thinking she is going to stand up. Edie is thinking she is going to stand up. The man stopped throwing up and now he is slumped.

Edie pokes him and he moves a little, makes a noise. Edie is thinking of getting home to Beau, and the only way to get home to Beau and pat her hand along his broad flank and feel his steady heartbeat beneath her fingers is to stand up and climb over bodies and yell if she has to: "Let me out! Let me out!" Edie is thinking she is going to stand up.

Sheldon is thinking yes, here, now people are done trying to be human. People are crying and retching and howling, and loudly. They are pure being. Which is the whole point: to get them past their thresholds and beyond any sense of what they are and what they could bear. The point is that they are everything and nothing and can bear it all. They will leave the sweat lodge awed by their own power, made huge by their fortitude. They will rush Sheldon in the lobby later, they will run up with their stacks of books, they will grab on without asking, they will hug him around the neck. They will love him.

Veronica thinks she is hallucinating when the slit of light grows and grows. Her brain can't make sense of the brightness. The brightness blinds.

Mommy keeps poking Gilbert. *Five more minutes, Mommy. Let me–*

Bette watches the darkness become people, everywhere around her gasping and blinking and stretching and it feels like—she can't say how and won't be able to describe it later and will stop even trying—birth.

Edie stops poking and starts shoving, though when she calls

out, it sounds the same as everyone calling out, of a piece, so many bodies now, so much new noise.

Sheldon stands at the opening, shepherding each lurching and shambolic person, one by one, their hair and clothing drenched, their faces fiery. They are crying, humming, sobbing, cheering. Each stops to touch Sheldon, a hand to his face, a squeeze of his bicep or shoulder, more than one grasping hug. More than two. More than three.

Veronica has never seen such a beautiful sidewalk. Such beautiful fogged windows from the indoor pool. Such beautiful Ramada Inn and Suites parking lot.

Bette mistakes the screaming for joy at the world made whole again.

Edie is screaming.

Sheldon is looking at the slumped body and the screaming woman and he is telling himself *go, go* though he too is gummy-legged and wrung-out, he too suffers. He is watching people running and stumbling to the slumped body—*go go*—watching them laying the body flat, pressing on the chest—yelling about doctor, about ambulance—*go!*—Sheldon flashing for the quickest of seconds on his first guru, the meditation weekend he'd been dragged to by the boyfriend on the cusp of breaking up with him, Sheldon's first business (QR-coded license plate holders and car accessories) newly failed, Clark (a hell of a guru name) guiding them all weekend to the breathing and the being that Sheldon could barely get ahold of, bouncing and restless and needing only his boyfriend

to bear-hug him and say the end was not imminent, Clark
spending all weekend doling out mantras like gifts, quietly
placing his hand on the head of a meditator and whispering
so hum to the woman spilling out of her spandex and *om
gam ganapataye namaha* to the very skinny older gentleman
with a gray ponytail and *lam-vam-ram-yam-ham-om* to
Sheldon's boyfriend, which Sheldon took to mean Clark and
his boyfriend were fucking or if they weren't fucking they
soon would be, Sheldon waiting and waiting and waiting and
waiting for his mantra, voracious for it, knowing he was doing
this all wrong and not caring, never wanting anything so bad
in his life, until Clark placed a hand on Sheldon's head and
whispered *om*, Sheldon trying not to be disappointed, trying
to hold on to *om* fast and fierce to make it his own, trying to
swallow the sound, but to his surprise, the sound swallowing
him, *om* a vibration inside his own head, *om* filling his cheeks,
om timed to his heartbeat, and oh my god was he doing, *om*
against his dark eyelids, *om* singing down his throat, *om* for a
brief and infinite second (gone as quick as it came, a second
he will spend a lifetime chasing) empty and everything and
warmth and wind and cock and coccyx, goddamn he was
doing, look at him doing, look at him.

the book of
adornments

THE WOMAN WHOSE NAME Viola has already
forgotten slides a fat three-ring binder across the table and
asks if Vi would like an adornment. The room is dressed in
landscape paintings and lightly patterned carpeting, aspiring
to the nowhereness of a hotel room or an office park.

"An adornment," Vi repeats back to the woman, and the
word is so funny like everything is so funny. The landscape
painting behind the woman is inartful mountains. It reminds
Vi of the man on PBS who had once felt like a secret but
turned out to be a meme. Now he was dead. Everyone was
dead, a remarkable fact for the way everyone else was not
and going and going and going through their days, wildly
outnumbered.

The three-ring binder has page after page of simple black
and white drawings–terrible clip art–separated by theme.
Sports, it says at the top of a page: a black and white figure
of a woman on water skis, man in a baseball uniform, man
with a fishing rod. There is a religion theme (so many crosses,
a few with clip art Jesus).

Loved ones can select a picture to be etched on the
gravestone, the woman beneath the terrible landscape says.

Vi, it appears from the woman's face, is to respond to this statement.

There is a family theme (crib, upright man with arm around upright woman, child in profile, running). There is a food theme (pie, candy cane, sandwich). It's so stupid, she can't stop turning the pages. Each page is sheathed in a plastic sleeve, and the fact that it was someone's job to put these pieces of paper one by one into the plastic sleeves is almost too much. The plastic sticks lightly together and has to be peeled apart. It's a childhood sound, a low, satisfying *chhhhh*, though she couldn't say from where in childhood, all of childhood a feeling and a lump. All of childhood a tumor.

There is an art theme (paint palette, frame on easel, bust of nonspecific head). An outdoors theme (fir tree, pup tent, hawk) and Vi is starting to reverse engineer, conjuring the person whose life is conveyed by an old-timey radio (entertainment theme) or fireplace (home theme), feeling sorry for that person and superior, so superior, but also envious, not of the ridiculously adorned but of the ridiculous adorner, a *loved one* who sat exactly where Vi is sitting, eye level to the same bad landscape painting, turning the same plastic pages, but with a person inside of them who they can match up to a motorcycle (vehicles theme) or laptop (work theme) or cat on rug (pet theme) and have it mean something.

"No," she finally says to the woman. She is sad to be at the last page, a final, desperate yawp, probably for people exactly like her, who'd found nothing but grist and irony. *Hobbies* it says at the top: muscle car, toolbox, kite, jigsaw puzzle, hiking poles, binoculars, notepad, bowling ball, violin, tri-fold map. "But I'll take the harpsicord and the gerbil for mine."

The woman beneath the bad landscape talks of family plots and discount pricing and the best planning is advance planning. There is no way to explain the joke, and Vi runs one finger over the plastic, thinking for a senseless second that her mother will crystallize inside her, intact and whole, instead of as a droop of disappointment at the corner of her lip; *I'm good, no I'm good* from the doorway of a room; three stubborn chin whiskers.

The woman beneath the bad landscape stops talking, and suddenly. Having figured out the joke, she is smiling, though her smile is not one that communicates *that is funny.* Her eyes are large, and green for the first time. She reaches for her book and pulls it back across the table so quickly, it skids a little. She closes the back flap with a dull *fut* and flips it over, front side up, ready for the next.

Vi will, she tells herself, weave her way through the rows of headstones outside this building and see who got what adornment, though she won't. She'll get in her rental car and figure out room service lunch and coordinate her brother's airport pickup and forget about the adornments entirely, even when her husband calls later and asks, 'How did it go at the cemetery?' because she feels everything deeply right now—it is something she will miss later after her mother is merely dead instead of newly dead—and then can't hang onto anything at all because the nature of being not dead means going onto the next thing and the next thing and the next, and room service is an outrageous $17 for a grilled cheese plus automatic 18% gratuity.

The book of adornments comes back to her though, randomly and for years. When she is wolfing down a ban mi during a too-short lunch hour, bad clip art ban mi appears in her mind (food theme); when she is applying stain stick to her son's grassy soccer shorts: stain stick (domesticity theme); when she is beside her husband in the bathroom mirror, watching the toothpaste foaming down his chin like a rabid dog: foamy chin (marriage theme). It haunts her. She never took herself for someone who'd be haunted, and if she'd taken herself as someone who'd be haunted, she'd have picked a different ghost: ghost (orphan theme).

acknowledgements

These ten stories span a career. Thank you to everyone at the University of Oregon MFA Program and the Wisconsin Institute of Creative Writing. To early readers and early writing groups: Caroline, Jamie, Sarah, and Melissa. To the editors at the journals that made homes for these stories. To the incomparable Debra Gwartney; go read her books next.

To Dan Deweese for your belief in this collection and your beautiful books.

To Playa (Carrie Hardison and Deb Ford, superstars both), Kimmel Harding Nelson, Wildacres, and Hypatia in the Woods for the time to write and for restoring my writerly soul.

To Evan Morgan Williams and Jenny Noyce for their careful eyes on these pages. Any mistakes here are mine.

To everyone from Oak Drive who generously gave their time when I thought they would be my next book.

To Rebecca, Tim, Nora, Eliza, Cole, Lizzie Lou, Susanna, Madgrrls, Claudiac, McBee, Psim, Carolyn, Anna, tia, Courtney, Merideth, Alexis, Amy S., Amy P., Sophie, Paul C., Fred, Ellen, Herschel, Paul F., Esther, Eeta, and everyone who cheered me and my writing during the long, lean years.

To Jordan and Eli for home.

To Papa and Cai. Such great cheerleaders. I miss you.

about the author

Miriam Gershow is the author of *The Local News*, a finalist for the Ken Kesey Award for the Novel. She is the recipient of a Fiction Fellowship from the Wisconsin Institute for Creative Writing and an Oregon Literary Fellowship. Her stories appear in literary journals and anthologies. She lives with her family in Eugene, Oregon, where she teaches and writes.